NINE NIGHTS

Bernardo Carvalho was born in Rio de Janeiro in 1960. He has been correspondent for *A Folha De São Paulo* in both Paris and New York. He is the author of a number of other novels – most recently *Mongolia* – winner of the Prêmio Jabuti, Brazil's most prestigious literary prize. *Nine Nights* is his first novel to be published in English. Bernardo Carvalho lives in São Paulo.

BERNARDO CARVALHO

Nine Nights

TRANSLATED BY
Benjamin Moser

Published by Vintage 2008

2 4 6 8 10 9 7 5 3 1

Copyright © Bernardo Carvalho 2002
This English translation © Benjamin Moser 2007

Bernardo Carvalho has asserted his right under the Copyright, Designs
and Patents Act 1988 to be identified as the author of this work

First published in Portuguese in Brazil under the title *Nove Noites* by
Editora Companhia das Letras in 2002

First published in Great Britain in 2007 by
William Heinemann
Random House, 20 Vauxhall Bridge Road,
London SW1V 2SA

www.vintage-books.co.uk

Addresses for companies within The Random House Group Limited can be
found at: www.randomhouse.co.uk/offices.htm

The Random House Group Limited Reg. No. 954009

A CIP catalogue record for this book
is available from the British Library

ISBN 9780099470335

The Random House Group Limited makes every effort to ensure
that the papers used in its books are made from trees that have
been legally sourced from well-managed and credibly certified forests.
Our paper procurement policy can be found at:
www.rbooks.co.uk/environment

Mixed Sources
Product group from well-managed
forests and other controlled sources
www.fsc.org Cert no. TT-COC-2139
© 1996 Forest Stewardship Council
FSC

Printed in the UK by CPI Bookmarque, Croydon, CR0 4TD

To the memory of Fábio T. Carvalho
and for Mariza Corrêa

1

This is for when you get here. You have to be prepared. Somebody has to warn you. You are entering a place where truth and lies no longer have the meanings they had outside. Just ask the Indians. Anything. Whatever crosses your mind. And tomorrow, when you wake up, ask them again. And then the day after tomorrow. Each time the same question. And every day you'll get a different answer. The truth is lost among all the contradictions and absurdities. When you come looking for something the past has already buried, you need to know that you're in a place where memories are lost for ever. Secrets are the only things we can take to our graves, and, like you and me, they are the only inheritance left behind. They wait to be assigned some meaning, even if they conceal no mystery at all. But our curiosity about these presumed mysteries relies on their lack of meaning. The story rests on facts that must have seemed unquestionable. That the American anthropologist Buell Quain, my friend, died on the night of 2 August 1939, aged twenty-seven. That he killed himself for no apparent reason, in an inopportune act of terrifying violence. That he did so despite the pleas of the two Indians who accompanied him on his final day, as he returned from the village to Carolina. And that they fled, appalled by the horror and the blood. That he slashed himself and then hanged himself. That he left remarkable letters that explained nothing. That he was described as unhappy and deranged in reports I myself had the misfortune to help write, in order to avert an official inquiry. I have spent years waiting for you, whoever you are. I have only told the things I know for sure. But I can no longer trust to luck and risk having my memory disappear along with myself. Nor can I entrust to unknown hands things that are properly yours, things that during all these years of sadness and disillusionment I have kept under lock and key, waiting for you. Forgive me. I can't take the risk. I am no longer young enough or strong enough to face down death. Tomorrow I'm taking the boat back to Carolina. But before I go I am leaving this testimonial, for whenever you arrive to confront this absolute chaos.

Welcome. They're going to tell you that the suicide was all very abrupt and unexpected. That it took everyone by surprise. They'll tell you all sorts of things. I know what you expect of me. And what you must be thinking. But don't ask me for things I never found myself, facts in black and white, precise times and dates. All you can go on is the imponderable, the fragility of what I have to tell you, just as I had to depend on the stories the Indians told, and Professor Pessoa's uncertain translations. Stories rely on the trust of the person hearing them, and that person's ability to interpret them. And when you come you'll be on your guard. Dr Buell, in his way, was also sceptical. He resisted as much as he could. We need reasons to believe. Would I be abusing your patience and tolerance, whoever you are, if I reminded you that we shall all die? I remember the day in March 1939 when he arrived in a city he described in his letters as dead. The first time I saw him he was as sceptical as you are now. Everyone recognized the rumble of the Condor seaplane as it approached the city. Nobody else visited us. Lots of people ran down to the river. I was busy working, but I could still see the shadow of the plane on the floor of the roofless house, as it flew over the mango trees on its way to the river. I finished what I was doing and went down to the port. He was posing for the photographer the Condor agent had hired to commemorate the event. With his camera mounted on a tripod, the photographer immortalized the illustrious ethnologist's arrival. Together with the Indians and the pilot, the visitor stood on the wing of the plane. His arrival provoked a sensation that five months later had nonetheless already been forgotten, if that's what you want to know. We so quickly grow accustomed to the extraordinary. I'm the only one who remembers him now. But on that day, neither I nor anyone else in town could have imagined what we were getting. He arrived in a white hat, like the captain of a ship, a white shirt, wide, loose trousers, and boots. Neither I nor anyone else could see past his elegance, so loftily inappropriate for the place and the occasion, and even more so when I look back on it now. Nobody could have foreseen the disaster that in less than five months would end his life. I moved closer to the scene the city was mutely watching, not understanding the mission it was welcoming, a mission no human soul could have turned away. I was that soul. The Condor agent introduced us, but the ethnologist didn't register me. He shook my hand like any other and smiled, smiled at everyone, but he didn't notice me. He hardly heard my name. If he had, he certainly would have made a joke, because he did have a sense of humour, after all. People always laugh at my name. And he had just arrived. Only later would he understand what he had got himself into, and the advantages of an alliance with me. Only then would he accept my friendship, when he had no other. I might be from the back of beyond, a friend of the Indians, but I am educated and I am not a fool. I don't hold grudges, especially not against Dr Buell, my friend, despite everything he might have thought or written. My only access to his writings was via Professor Pessoa's uncertain translations, when I rooted through the dead man's papers in search of an explanation, papers that I myself did my best to hide. I didn't need anyone to find a meaning. You can't let the dead take over from those who remain. I couldn't have predicted the tragedy. From the beginning, though, I was the only one who could see the desperation in his eyes, the desperation he was trying, not always successfully, to hide. And I guessed at his motives before they were revealed, though I preferred to ignore them, or pretend to, if only to take some of the pressure off him. In that way, I believe, I aided him as best I could. During those few times when he could no longer contain himself, I had been there, and I knew that for him my silence was the proof of my friendship. That's how men are. Or do you think that when we looked at each other we weren't aware that we were both trying to hide the same thing? Nothing is more valuable than the trust of a friend. That is why I appreciate the Indians, among whom I have lived since childhood, ever since my grandfather pacified them. I always welcomed them into my home. I always knew what they said about me behind my back, that they thought I was a little crazy, not so different from all white people. But the important thing, for me, is that they could count on me. And that they knew I didn't expect anything in return. They would get anything they wanted from me, and God knows their demands are endless. I did everything I could. And for Dr Buell as well. I gave him exactly what I gave the Indians. The same friendship. Because he, like them, was alone, unprotected. Regardless of what he thought or wrote, he was no more than a boy. He could have been my son. Nothing in my life has upset me as much. Not even when I was fired from my job as chief of the Manoel da Nóbrega Indian Liaison Post by Mr Cildo Meireles, inspector of the Indian Protection Service, three years after the tragedy, when he recommended that I ought to leave my heart five leagues from the Post, and took me away from the Indians for good – he didn't want me around. Not even the humiliation of having been removed from the position I had held for a little more than a year and which, to help defend the Indians, Dr Buell himself had helped me get, sending letters of recommendation to Rio de Janeiro. And not even the massacre of the village of Cabeceira Grossa, which Dr Buell might have been able to prevent had he still been alive, if he had still been among them when the great landholders ambushed the Indians a year after his suicide. Nothing saddened me as much as the death of my friend, whose memory I decided to honour. I greeted him when he arrived. I have no regrets about anything I have thought or written. I asked for nothing in return, because I know that, deep down, I was the last person he could depend on.

I left the roofless house at dusk, just as a cloud of bats departed the hollowed-out trunk of a mango tree. They hurled through the streets in a torrent, a blind, sweeping flight, oblivious to both bicycles and pedestrians. In that dead city (his words, if we can trust Professor Pessoa's translations) the pedestrians were as oblivious to the bats as the bats were to them. I may be ignorant, but I was never superstitious. The cloud of little vampires that greeted him may have been an ill omen. But when I reached the riverbank all I saw were his eyes, the expression they had taken on, out of distraction and fatigue, between one photograph and the next, when he forgot that others were looking at him. He wanted to go to the village. He was exhausted. He wanted to escape the gaze of others. Only you can tell me what he had come to do here, if he really came to die, as I ended up suspecting when I received the news of the suicide. For years I've been waiting, in vain.

Towards the end of the afternoon of the 9th of August, five months after his arrival in Carolina, twenty Indians arrived in the city. They brought the sad news and, in their baggage, Dr Buell's personal items, which I myself, with tears in my eyes, received and catalogued: two music books, a Bible, a pair of shoes, a pair of slippers, three pairs of pyjamas, six shirts, two ties, a black cloak, a towel, four handkerchiefs, two pairs of socks, a pair of suspenders, two linen suits, two worsted suits, two pairs of underwear, and an envelope of photographs. His picture was not among them. There was a picture of a wooden house on a beach; of the blacks of the South Pacific, who had told him legends and sung him songs; of the Trumai of the Upper Xingu; but there were no pictures of his family, neither of his father, nor of his mother, nor of his sister, nor of any woman. He might have burned them along with the letters he had received before he killed himself. The Indians hadn't touched anything. They came directly to my house without stopping or speaking to anyone along the way – they were frightened, fearful of being incriminated. That didn't prevent the news from spreading, and before long a small crowd had gathered in front of my modest dwelling. I sent for Professor Pessoa at once. He, after reading one of the letters the unfortunate man had left behind, in English, calmed the Indians and affirmed that they had no responsibility for the tragedy. There were letters addressed to the United States, to Rio de Janeiro, to Mato Grosso, and two for Carolina: one for Captain Ângelo Sampaio, chief of police, and another for me.

Since then I have waited for you, whoever you are. I know that you will come to claim your property, the letter he wrote to you before killing himself and which, for safety's sake, forgive me, I kept. I was wary. I had my suspicions, but I couldn't understand it, and I didn't want to take the chance of asking Professor Pessoa to translate it for me. It was the only one I didn't send on to Rio de Janeiro. Now, barely six years have passed since Dr Buell's death, and the professor himself has announced that he is an ethnologist, a self-proclaimed student of the Krahô. He acts as if no ethnologist had ever set foot in Carolina, placing himself on a level with a man who didn't know him and who claimed not to remember who he was. From his perspective that is only logical, since recalling the memory of that man would only throw his mediocrity and ignorance into sharper relief. I myself may be from the back of beyond, but I'm not a fool. Of the sealed envelopes, that was the only one not addressed to Dr Buell's family, or to an anthropologist or missionary. Please understand. Those were tough times. I did it all out of friendship, out of a desire to protect him. You can't imagine, whoever you are. The letters went to Rio de Janeiro before they were sent to the United States. Nothing could guarantee that they wouldn't be opened and read. That's what the Maranhão State authorities did when they brought them to Professor Pessoa for an explanation. Or they might have been lost in the post. An inquiry may have brought still other risks. So I kept that last letter with me, to protect him, and the Indians. I swore that no one other than you would ever lay eyes on it. I sent you a note in place of the letter, in code, it's true, which Professor Pessoa helped me draft in English. He didn't know to whom I was writing or why. He thought the note was meant for one of the dead man's relatives, since I had asked for his help once before with a letter of condolence to his mother. I could never be sure that you received the note, or that you understood it, since you didn't come. I have been waiting for years, but I can't take the chance, and I no longer have the strength to stare death in the face. Tomorrow I'm taking the boat back to Carolina. Before that, I'm leaving this, for when you get here.

2

Nobody ever asked me. So I never had to reply. I can't
pretend that I'd never heard of him, but I had no idea who
he was until I read the name of Buell Quain for the first
time. It was in a newspaper article, on the morning of
Saturday, 12 May 2001, almost sixty-two years after his
death on the eve of the Second World War. The article
appeared months before another war began. Today, wars
seem like intermittent episodes, though in fact they never
cease. I read the same paragraph several times and repeated
the name out loud to make sure I wasn't dreaming. Finally
I understood – or confirmed, I no longer know – that I
had heard it before. The article mentioned the letters of
another anthropologist, who had also died among the
Brazilian Indians, in circumstances that were still the
subject of academic debate. And in a single sentence, it
made a parallel to the case of 'Buell Quain, who committed
suicide among the Krahô Indians in August 1939'.

I sought out the anthropologist who had written the
article. At first, on the telephone, she was curt. She must
have thought it odd that someone would call her over such
a small detail in her article, but she didn't mention that.
We exchanged a few emails, and that gradually brought us
closer. She preferred not to meet me in person. She wanted
to be sure my motives were not academic. But even if, at

the beginning, she apparently distrusted my interest in the man, she didn't enquire as to my real intentions. At least she didn't insist on knowing why I was interested. She supposed that I wanted to write a novel, that my interest was literary, and I didn't contradict her. The story really was remarkable. Slowly, as my questions took me deeper into the case, she began to believe that my curiosity about the suicidal ethnologist was only natural. Perhaps she was only being discreet. Or perhaps she felt that, in some way, because of some experience she herself could not imagine, I too saw something in that case, something that she later revealed she had always suspected, when we finally met and she put the question to me. She gave me the first clues.

The papers were scattered among archives in Brazil and the United States. I made a few trips, a few contacts, and slowly started putting together the puzzle, creating an image of the man I sought. Many people helped me. Nothing depended on my actions; the whole story depended on a combination of coincidences that began on the day I read, to my shock, the anthropologist's article in the paper and, after sounding that name out loud, first heard it in my own voice.

Buell Quain killed himself on the night of 2 August 1939 – the same day Albert Einstein sent President Roosevelt the historic letter alerting him to the possibility of an atomic bomb, and three weeks before Hitler and Stalin signed their Non-Aggression Pact, the green light for the Second World War and, for many, one of the greatest political disenchantments of the twentieth century. By a straightforward coincidence, I came across a reference to Einstein's letter as soon as I started to investigate Quain's death. He never knew about it. His world was not my own. He didn't see the world, he didn't see the bomb – even though, in the delirium of his final observations of the Krahô, and drawing on his recollections of the popular science magazines he had read in adolescence, he tried to apply 'the same mathematical principles that govern atomic phenomena' to social phenomena, detecting in the Indians 'cultural comportment syndromes' analogous to the laws of physics. He had an almost adolescent fascination with science and technology. He could not have believed that the more a man struggles to escape death the closer he gets to self-destruction. It couldn't have occurred to him that this might just be the traitorous, hidden scheme of science, its rebuttal: though much of what he saw among the Indians, and intuitively associated with his own experience, might have drawn him close. When he killed himself, he was trying to return, on foot, from the village of Cabeceira Grossa to Carolina, situated at the border of Maranhão with what was then part of Goiás and today is the state of Tocantins. He was twenty-seven years old. He left at least seven letters, which he wrote, in tears, in his final hours. He wanted to leave the world in an orderly fashion, to judge by the contents of the four letters I saw, addressed to his thesis adviser, Ruth Benedict, of Columbia University in New York; to Mrs Heloísa Alberto Torres, director of the National Museum in Rio de Janeiro; to

Manoel Perna, an engineer in Carolina who had become his friend; and to Captain Ângelo Sampaio, police chief of the same city. He wanted to clear the Indians of any possible suspicion, name the executors of his will, and instruct them as to the disposition of his property. The letters tell the living how to carry on after his death. Among those I did not manage to find, however, was at least one addressed to his father, a physician, Dr Eric P. Quain, who had recently divorced and was then living in the Annex Hotel in Bismarck, North Dakota. Another was sent to the Reverend Thomas Young, an American missionary based, with his wife, in Taunay, in Mato Grosso. He addressed a third to his brother-in-law, Charles C. Kaiser, who was married to his sister Marion. In those, he may have left more than instructions.

Quain arrived in Brazil in February 1938. He disembarked in Rio de Janeiro shortly before Carnival. He stayed in a boarding house in Lapa, an area of low-lifes and prostitutes. One year and five months later he was dead. When they heard the news, some of his colleagues at Columbia University, in New York, speculated that his journey had been part of a deliberate plan of suicide. Others thought he had been murdered. His stated intention was to study the Karajá Indians, continuing the recent work carried out by another Columbia anthropologist, William Lipkind, and his wife. Quain changed his plans when he got to Rio. The inaccessible Trumai Indians, on the Coliseu river in the Upper Xingu, were on the verge of extinction and represented a much greater challenge than the well-studied and acculturated Karajá. The young ethnologist, daring and ambitious, could not have expected the consequences of the challenge when he decided to focus on the Trumai instead. His solitary expedition to the Trumai was marked by unanticipated setbacks, frustrations, and obstacles which finally interrupted his field research. The unwillingness of the dictatorial Estado Novo to help him interrupted his field research and forced his return to Rio de Janeiro in February 1939. The blow further unsettled his already unstable mind.

His reluctant return to the capital coincided with the arrival in Brazil of a colleague from Columbia University, Charles Wagley, who had come to study the Tapirapé. It also coincided with Ruth Landes's passage through the city. The young woman anthropologist from New York had already been in the country for months, where she was studying the black population and the Candomblé religion of Bahia. All three were prize students of Ruth Benedict. Benedict was one of the leading representatives of the school of anthropology that linked Culture and Personality, attempting to explain behaviour in its social context and therefore relativize the concepts of normality and abnormality. In the mid-1930s, in the wake of the New Deal, Columbia's anthropology department, led by Franz Boas, attracted students with its liberal thinking and its ambition to use science to confront social prejudices. Interviews with her students and colleagues suggest Benedict preferred students who were out of tune with the society they belonged to, students somehow maladjusted to American culture. Perhaps recognizing something of herself in them, she protected them.

When the news of her student's suicide reached her, Benedict had retreated to the isolation of the Rocky Mountains, near the Canadian border, where she was beginning a sabbatical. She wrote to Quain's mother: 'My secretary just telegraphed me, and amidst my own pain all I can think about is you. He was a son that always concerned you. It's agonizing. Of all my students, Buell was the one I took most warmly to heart, and all I can think of now is the personal loss and mourn his suffering, the reasons for which we still don't understand. I will never forget his dedication to his work and I am happy that by publishing it I can help place him in the vanguard of field research. He achieved much, and I believe deep down he wanted to achieve much more. I am paralyzed by grief. May God comfort you in your suffering.'

Buell Quain was accepted into the Columbia graduate programme after earning a degree in zoology from the University of Wisconsin at Madison, in 1934. As an under-graduate, he had also shown an interest in several other subjects, principally literature and music. Quain's book *The Flight of the Chiefs* was published in 1942, after his death. It included transcriptions of the legends and songs he had collected in a village in Vanua Levu, in the Fiji Islands, during his first field expedition, when he was only twenty-four. In his preface, William Ellery Leonard, author of an English version of the Babylonian epic *Gilgamesh*, recalled that the ancient poem's themes of friendship, death, and the search for immortality had attracted Buell during his student years. Leonard praises his adventurous spirit, lists his former student's voyages, and laments his early death in the Brazilian interior. When he finished high school, aged sixteen, Buell had already crossed the United States by car. In 1929, before he entered university, he spent six months in Europe and the Middle East, visiting Egypt, Syria, and Palestine. The following year, over the summer holiday, he went to Russia. After passing his exams, in February 1931, he embarked on another six-month journey, working as a sailor on a boat bound for Shanghai. In 1935, he was in New York, and the following year in Fiji. In a letter to Buell's mother, months after the ethnologist's death, Heloísa Alberto Torres professed herself amazed by what he had done in such a short time. 'He was so young and had seen so much. What an extraordinary life!'

When a child is born, its parents, incredibly enough, greet their unknowable creation with blind euphoria. Full of hope, they transmute their incapacity to foresee the future, and the impotence of all their precautionary measures, into promising augurs. It has to be this way, to prevent the human race from disappearing from the face of the earth: otherwise it would have long since perished at the hands of zealous, murderous mothers. Buell Halvor Quain was born on 31 May 1912, at 11:53 at night, in the hospital at Bismarck, capital of North Dakota. His birth certificate affirms that the necessary measures were taken against neonatal ophthalmia, a then-customary procedure intended to prevent the transmission of venereal diseases to newborns. Almost five years after his suicide, his mother wrote to Heloísa Alberto Torres on 31 May 1944: 'He was born thirty-two years ago tonight. As a little boy, he always answered people who asked when he was born: "At ten minutes to June." Five years ago, he sent me his last birthday letter, from Carolina.'

Eric P. Quain, Buell's father, was forty-one when his son was born. He was a surgeon. Born in Sweden, he was a Midwestern medical pioneer. He graduated in 1898 and brought modern surgical techniques to Bismarck, along with its first x-ray machine. The clinic he founded in 1907 is still one of the principal medical centres in the area. It only very recently changed its name from the Quain and Ramstad Clinic.

Fannie Dunn Quain was thirty-eight. It was her third birth, her second successful one. The couple already had a daughter, Marion. Like her husband, Fannie was a doctor, and graduated from the University of Michigan at Ann Arbor in 1898. She was the first woman from North Dakota to be awarded a medical degree. When she married, on 25 March 1903, she abandoned her profession to become a homemaker. Throughout her life, she was active in public service, especially in matters related to health and education. When Buell was born, she was a member of the educators' board of Bismarck High School. She campaigned for a tuberculosis asylum in the state, and participated in the Democratic convention of 1936.

Fannie and Eric Quain separated shortly before their son's suicide. Apparently unable to accept Buell's death – despite what his daughter Marion would later reveal to Ruth Benedict in a strange, bitter letter – the father pulled some strings and got an influential North Dakota senator, Gerald Nye, to ask the State Department for an investigation. The request went nowhere, since the evidence of suicide was irrefutable.

After his son's death, Eric Quain moved to the West Coast, where his daughter's family also spent time, at least over the Christmas holidays. There are signs, however, that father and daughter were not always on good terms. He remarried and continued to practise medicine until his death, in Salem, Oregon, in 1962. Fannie Quain struggled to conquer her loneliness, her memories of her son, and the difficulty of living amidst 'the things he brought back from all over the world'. At first, she tried to stay away from home, so as not to have to live with the eloquent silence of those objects, beginning with his piano, which was 'the thing he loved best, and which now is silent'. In 1939, she and her daughter travelled to Chicago and Oregon, where they spent Christmas near Mount Hood, outside Portland. She visited relatives in California. Above all, she had a mission. With the help of Ruth Benedict, she published his notes from Fiji (there was, besides *Flight of the Chiefs*, another narrative record of his ten months, in 1935 and 1936, spent among the indigenous people of Vanua Levu, which was published in 1948 under the title *Fijian Village*). She also studied linguistics in order to prepare for publication her son's manuscripts on the language of the Krahô. In her correspondence with Heloísa Alberto Torres, one can see that she was greatly distressed. It was a difficult moment. She was suddenly alone in the world, divorced, her son dead. And her letters betray a strange anxiety, as if, more than wanting to know the reason her son killed himself, she feared that somebody was on to her, would find her out. She died in 1950, aged seventy-six.

In letters written two months before his suicide, the anthropologist mentioned that 'family matters' forced him to suspend his work with the Indians and return to the United States. He wrote to Heloísa on 5 June 1939:

The two *contos de réis* you sent facilitate my return to New York, via Bahia or Belém. As much as I would like to come back to Rio de Janeiro, family matters in the United States demand my attention. I have already mentioned sickness in the family, but that is not the problem now. My parents have just been through a divorce that lasted six months. They are almost seventy and have hated each other for at least thirty years. My father suffers from an acute form of senile degeneration – perhaps that is what has led him over the last six months to dig through the past. You might find this materialistic of me, but I need to return in the hopes of rescuing a small piece of property that I can place at the service of ethnology. But I fear it may be too late.

Heloísa Alberto Torres was an active, powerful woman. She was large, very pale, and had blue-rinsed hair, according to Alfred Métraux, a Swiss anthropologist specializing in Latin America, who had made several trips to Brazil. In her youth, she must have been an interesting woman. She came from a wealthy family in the state of Rio de Janeiro. She had always been close to power. As Director of the National Museum, she managed to maintain her influence and retain her position throughout the duration of the Estado Novo. An arrangement between Columbia and the National Museum had placed her in charge of the four young American anthropologists then in Brazil – Quain himself, Charles Wagley, Ruth Landes, and William Lipkind. Buell had originally planned to go to the Karajá with Lipkind. Among the letters he wrote in the hours before his suicide, one was addressed to Heloísa. Up to that point, she had been a kind of mother hen, protective but sometimes domineering, to the young Columbia ethnologists. It is not hard to imagine what she felt upon reading these lines:

Dear Heloísa,

I am dying of a contagious disease. You will receive this letter after my death. The letter should be disinfected. I asked for my notes and my tape recorder (sorry, but without any recordings) to be sent to the Museum. Please, forward the notes to Columbia.

Don't think the worst of me. I appreciated your

friendship. But I cannot complete the catalogue of the collection that the Indians are going to pack and send to you. I asked for the two *contos de réis* to be returned to you, because of my failure. However, if you decide to keep anything for the collection, please remember the Indians and send whatever you think appropriate to Manoel Perna, in Carolina.

I hope that Lipkind and Wagley live up to your expectations.

Sincerely,
Buell Quain

On 31 July, when he left the village, he hired two Indian boys, João and Ismael, as guides. They told Manoel Perna, an engineer in Carolina and the ethnologist's only friend there, that on the second day, at sunset, still ninety kilometres from their destination, Quain Buele – as they called him in the white man's tongue; Cãmtwỳon as he was known in Krahô – decided to spend the night near a swamp. He asked to stop, saying he was tired and could not go on. According to the Indians, there were no signs of physical illness. The disease was psychological. He had been infected for several days, since he had received his last news from home.

In the letter he sent Heloísa on 12 August 1939, confirming the telegram he had sent the night before to report Quain's suicide, Manoel Perna wrote: 'How terrible that his death came so painfully. We still don't know what led him to it. But according to reliable sources, we can infer that it was a response to family problems. The Indians say that after he received letters from his parents and family a few days ago, he had been very angry. He even told them that the news was very unpleasant before he tore up the letters and burned them.'

3

This is for when you get here. It was only for nine nights. If I claimed to have no idea why he had been motivated to suicide, it was only to avoid an inquest. The police investigated the case, took note of the facts, and described his mortal remains, at the request of the Americans. Don't get me wrong. I wouldn't have been able to explain anything. I carried the silence with me for many years, while I was waiting for you. Now I can't risk letting it all disappear with me. Of course, if I had known what was in the letters that he received before he killed himself, I would never have sent my brother to the village with them. The letters arrived at the beginning of July, when Dr Buell had already returned to the Indians. Weeks before, he had made his second visit to Carolina, to collect money and provisions, but above all – though he didn't say this to me – because he was afraid to spend his birthday in the village. I would have gone myself, if I had known that one of those letters contained a death sentence. I would have gone alone and on foot if need be, to bring him safely back to the city. He made me promise that I would have the letters sent by a porter as soon as they arrived. He was waiting for an answer. And I no longer have any doubt that this was the answer he was so anxiously awaiting. I know that I left him full of doubts, but I can guarantee you that he got his answer. Before I gave my brother that last mail shipment, which arrived at the beginning of July on the Condor plane, I noted a return address. I would later recognize the same address among the letters he wrote in the hours just before his death. That was the letter I decided to keep, the letter that he left for you. Whatever you may think, I did it out of respect for Dr Buell's memory, and to protect the Indians. The Indians said that he fell into a terrible self-absorption after receiving those last letters, an attitude otherwise unknown during his time in the village. These were the letters he burned on the last day of his trip back to Carolina. The light he needed to write his final letters came from that little fire. He was sobbing profusely, and after he was done, in the middle of the night, he committed suicide. But nobody ever knew what was in that letter. When he decided to leave and communicated his resolution to the Indians ('I have already asked the clouds to take me out of here and nothing happened,' he supposedly told an Indian woman. I'm not asking you to believe anything – the truth depends entirely on the listener's trust), he said he had received bad news from home. He told some that his father had left his mother, who was elderly and had no means of support. But if he had already spoken of that to me on his last trip to Carolina, that could not have been the bad news. He told others that his wife had betrayed him with his brother – but I knew very well that he didn't have a brother. He didn't mention any illness. He didn't want to frighten the Indians. He saved the excuse that he had a contagious disease for the whites, asking them to disinfect the letters before reading them. That at least was the reason he gave Heloísa and, as I later learned, his professor in the United States.

That was the reason he gave in the letter he sent to me as well, knowing full well I would keep my mouth shut. Nobody other than me ever knew about the letter he left you. I have been waiting for all these years. Now, to the weight of silence, there is the weight of guilt. But back then I didn't have a choice. After a few days, everything was forgotten, and the city returned to its habitual calm. It's hard to believe. The same men who, five months before, had bombarded the American ethnologist with invitations to the opening festivities of the Casa Humberto de Campos, nicknamed the Backwoods Academy of Letters, now barely remembered his name, or that he had ever been in the city. The wise men of Carolina. Who am I to say what I think? They think I'm ignorant, but I'm not a fool. I'll show them respect if that's what they want. The man who arrived on that sluggish March afternoon was tormented. The evening before his return to the village, he was apprehensive. And I no longer know if it was because he didn't know what to expect there or precisely because he did. Sometimes, I wonder when he started to imagine what nobody there possibly could. I marvel at how far he had come to die. Yet he did go to the intellectuals' party. Uncomfortable with the small crowd, he wore a troubled expression. The entire city gathered to hear the speeches establishing the literary society. He couldn't see me among the crowds swarming around the school, pressing against the doors and windows, trying to hear, without understanding, what was being said inside. But that was where, for the second time, I got a glimpse of his eyes.

4

Nobody ever asked me, so I never had to reply. Everyone wonders what it is that suicides know. At first, I let myself be taken in by the easy supposition that the death could only have been the result of some secret passion. I conducted my search along those lines. There must have been someone else involved. No one is completely alone in the world. There had to be a letter that revealed his desires and feelings. On the morning of 8 March 1939, while he was waiting for the mules and the provisions for the six-day trek to the village of Cabeceira Grossa, Quain, seated at his typewriter, caught up with his correspondence. He thought he would isolate himself in the village for a period of three months. He couldn't count on a messenger or a porter showing up. He didn't plan to return to Carolina before June. I read three of these letters. The longest was addressed to Ruth Landes, his Columbia colleague in Brazil studying Candomblé. The other two were directed to Heloísa and her assistant, Maria Júlia Pourchet, whom he had met in Rio de Janeiro. In his letter to the director of the National Museum, Quain kept to practical matters, reporting his registering with the police in São Luís, the money he had sent, and the expenses he had incurred in buying gifts for the Indians. He delicately described his first impressions of Carolina to Maria Júlia Pourchet.

I wasn't aware of this letter until it was suggested that I look up a professor of anthropology at the University of São Paulo. Her aunt, also an anthropologist and already deceased, had visited Quain's mother in the United States in 1940, shortly after his death. I found her phone number and called the professor. She didn't know anything of her aunt's supposed visit to Fannie Quain, but she told me something I could hardly have guessed, exactly what I was keenest to discover when I first spoke to her of Buell Quain. 'He and my mum had a little flirtation, long before I was born, of course,' she said, immediately on hearing that unusual name.

The answer left me speechless, all the more so because I had been attempting to discover, without success, if he had a wife. He claimed that he was married in a letter to the president of the Brazilian Supervisory Committee for Artistic and Scientific Expeditions. This was in February 1938, when he had first arrived in the country and was requesting authorization for his field work. But no other document, from before or after his death, referred to a wife.

For a moment I didn't know what to say. 'But he was married!' I ventured. To which the professor replied, partly offended, partly indignant: 'No, he wasn't. At least, that is not how he represented himself in Rio de Janeiro. Nor how he introduced himself to my mother.'

I thought that a love story would explain everything. We arranged to meet at the university, where she confirmed what she had said on the phone. Before I could reach for the letter, she made a point of reading it out loud, in English. She punctuated her reading with pauses and intonations, emphasizing phrases she found significant with raised eyebrows. But they meant nothing to me:

Dear Miss Júlia,

This is just a note. I am leaving for a Krahô village in about two hours. We're waiting for trousers and shirts. It's going to be me and a group of Krahô Indians who were in Carolina when we arrived. The trousers and shirts are for them. I don't like to give them clothes, since they are better off without them – but they insist.

Yesterday evening, I went to a party in honor of Humberto de Campos. There were about ten brief speeches about his life and work. I was surprised by the interest the people of Carolina had for literary subjects. They flocked to the doors and crowded at the windows to hear what was said. I could only understand half of it, but I was impressed by the audience's serious interest.

The professor also showed me a picture of Quain. I had already seen it in the Heloísa Alberto Torres archives; he had given a copy to the professor's mother. He sits in a chair facing the camera, wearing a white shirt. He has an ironic, defiant expression. There is a dedication on the reverse of the original. Nothing hinting at their flirtation, of course. That's what they called it back then. Mum spoke of him often. He was a very good-looking man, tall, dark, different from your normal American. When they said goodbye, before he got on the plane, he promised her he would think things over. You know what I mean, yes? He was going to seriously consider the possibility of an engagement,' she said, still refusing to let me touch the letter.

The professor could not have suspected why I was so eager for a copy of the document, and why my mouth had been nervously smiling ever since she started reading it aloud. On the one hand the 'note' was a disappointment to me, since, despite what she said, it contained no proof of a love affair. On the other hand, I had just learned who Miss Júlia was. He had mentioned the name in another letter, written the same morning, before he left for the village. A month before, I had received a copy from a Canadian researcher. Quain was in Carolina, waiting for his mules and his provisions, when he wrote to Ruth Landes. He reported the same information he had communicated to Maria Júlia Pourchet, but he saw them through different eyes, and described them in different words. He was more sarcastic, more truthful, and more honest, with the intimacy, concern, and desperation of a man opening up to a friend:

Dear Ruth,

Carolina is a tedious place – illiterates and intellec-tuals. The intellectuals wear white suits and ties and belong to the literary society. I joined them at a meeting in honor of Humberto de Campos, the great poet of the Maranhão. There were ten speakers: the life of the poet in ten parts. Including: Humberto the moralist; Humberto the humanitarian; Humberto the humorist; and finally Humberto the philosopher. It could all have been very nice if it hadn't been so ridiculously pompous. And finally it was somewhat disappointing to hear a young lawyer from Rio de Janeiro (he probably went to school in Rio or something like that; I think he's from the north) say that 'we cannot speak of Humberto the philosopher without recalling how much he suffered. Humberto, the sufferer . . .' And then it was revealed that he was a stoic, since he was always smiling. This last speaker got the warmest applause.

I met a group of Krahô Indians and they seemed fearfully obtuse. They have funny hairstyles, pierced ears, and still don't wear clothes in the cities.

There are a lot of things about Brazilians and Brazilian cities that make me want to rip off my clothes and masturbate in public. But I try to control myself. Seriously, you can't be honest, even with relatively sophisticated people, like Miss Júlia. And I'm furious with you for talking so much about me with her.

What was it that Buell Quain so badly wanted to hide?

5

Professor Luiz de Castro Faria met me in Niterói towards the end of the afternoon. I was returning from the Heloísa Alberto Torres archives in Itaboraí. It was dreadfully hot. Castro Faria is one of the last people alive who met Quain in Brazil. We spoke in the library of his apartment in Icaraí. In 1938, aged twenty-four, he participated in the historic expedition to the Serra do Norte. He was an anthropologist from the National Museum and a member of the Supervisory Committee. From 6 June to 14 December, he accompanied Lévi-Strauss through the Mato Grosso all the way to Porto Velho, a journey that is in large part documented in *Tristes tropiques*, which immediately became an anthropological classic. The Estado Novo required the presence of a Brazilian scientist on all foreign expeditions, as a way of keeping an eye on them. Lévi-Strauss himself, with a certain antipathy, referred to the observer as a 'tax inspector'. There is a photo from 1939 in which Heloísa appears seated on a bench in the gardens of the National Museum, with Charles Wagley, Raimundo Lopes, and Edison Carneiro to her right and Claude Lévi-Strauss, Ruth Landes, and Luiz de Castro Faria to her left. Today, all but Castro Faria and Lévi-Strauss are dead. But even at that time there was an absence in the picture, which I only noticed after I began investigating the story of Buell

Quain. At that point, he was still alive and working among the Krahô. The image is a kind of portrait of him, through his absence. In every photograph there is a phantasmagoric element. But it is even more pronounced in this one. Everyone in the picture knew Buell Quain, and at least three of them took to their graves things that I will never be able to learn. In my obsession, I even found myself holding the picture in my hand, fascinated, my eyes glazed over, trying in vain to shake an answer from the eyes of Wagley, Heloísa, or Ruth Landes.

At eighty-eight, Castro Faria is lucid, very articulate, and in possession of a memory often sharper than my own – though like anybody else's it can be distorted by subjective impressions. He spoke of Quain for more than an hour, without growing tired. At the beginning, he was more reticent. The two were not quite friends: 'My relations with him were superficial. He always treated me very well. We weren't close. Since I didn't spend much time with him – we only met occasionally – I don't know anything about his private life. Quain wasn't especially close to Wagley, I don't think. They were the same age. They were both from Columbia, so they had a certain background in common. They were all students of Franz Boas's, which left its impression. Boas prized his best students. He was the pioneer of American anthropological research in Brazil. Wagley was my age. We were always together. He was my friend, a really close friend. He was always in Brazil. He married a Brazilian. We called him Chuck. He did his military service during the war, as a public service technician.

Nobody was that upset by Quain's death. Not even his Columbia colleagues. It's uncommon in America, where people are very individualistic, for them to get upset about things like that. Heloísa was, because she was responsible for his research. That was a heavy responsibility in those days, because you had to justify everything to the government, which exercised rigid control over research. The organs of repression were very active.' As he spoke, I remembered something I had seen only hours before, among Heloísa's papers in the archives of her house in Itaboraí. There was a letter, dating from weeks after Quain's death, in which she reproached the police chief of Carolina, Captain Ângelo Sampaio, as if he were her student or employee. She was very annoyed, exasperated at her own powerlessness over her compatriots' sluggishness and incompetence. Her repeated requests for Quain's belongings, which had been impounded by the Maranhão police, had had no effect. That left her in an even more awkward position in her dealings with the American authorities and the Columbia Anthropology Department. Her own authority was on the line. In the letter, she demanded once and for all the return of all the material Quain had left behind. And she told the captain that the case was becoming a 'national embarrassment'.

Playing dumb, I enquired as to his physical appearance. I had an idea what he looked like, but I was more interested in the impression he made, the reactions he provoked, than in his actual features. 'Nothing special. He was young, quite young.' Fat or thin? 'He wasn't fat, not at all. Nor was he particularly thin. He was just normal-looking.' Blond or dark? 'He wasn't light blond. I'd say his hair was a bit darker. Nothing remarkable.' Faced with the difficulty of getting anything out of the old professor, I decided to ask the opposite of what I wanted to know. 'Was he ugly?' 'No, I'd say he was actually rather good-looking, attractive.'

Slowly, Castro Faria became more comfortable in discussing the 'eccentricities' of his American colleague. He referred several times to the time Quain had taken him out for a grand dinner in Copacabana. The occasion had greatly impressed Castro Faria. 'I'm going to tell you a story. We'll probably never know if it's true. Wagley once told me that at Columbia he occasionally bought Quain lunch with his scholarship money. Only much later did he discover that the sponsor of the scholarship was none other than Buell Quain. The money was his. That's common in the United States, people contributing to charities. And that's how he was. They said he was very rich. His parents were doctors. He had a lot of money. But he hated using that. It was an obsession. He was very worried that people would see that he had means, so he went to great lengths to hide it. Once, to give you an idea, he took me to dinner at a very expensive restaurant in Copacabana, though he lived in a dive on the Rua do Riachuelo. To not spend money. He hated being rich.'

The question of his finances deserves attention. First of all, nothing indicates that Quain came from an especially wealthy background, though his parents were far from poor. They were successful Midwestern doctors.

During his field research in Brazil, the young ethnologist encountered genuine difficulties. In a letter to Heloísa dated 27 May 1939, he mentions his return to Carolina in search of funds:

> Now that the money has arrived, I feel stupid for having sent Ruth such a desperate plea. The people in Carolina have been very helpful and gave me all the credit I needed. But I prefer not to accumulate debts. I came back to Carolina without shoes and felt insecure about my shabby appearance. The only excuse I can think of is that it is important to dedicate all possible time to ethnological work. But I owe you and Dr Othon [Leonardos, a geologist at the National Museum] an explanation for not maintaining the social position that your letters provide me. I remain on good terms with Dr Othon's friends – but the poor figure I cut and my bad Portuguese intimidate me when I am with them. I'm sure they think my behavior makes me seem coarse.

Quain's main legacy was a life-insurance policy and his own savings. Incredibly enough, after he died, almost all of the correspondence between Heloísa, Manoel Perna, Ruth Benedict, his mother, and his sister focused on the question of his money. Nobody seemed to want to touch it. They were keen to pass it on as he had provided in his will. Years later, in an absurd departmental intrigue, Ruth Benedict's enemies accused her of having sent Quain to Brazil with the express intention of inheriting his fortune, as if she had foreseen her student's death and had prior knowledge of his decision to leave his money to a research fund, which she herself would administer. Many of the letters the dead man left behind were concerned with this question, and no other. In the case of Wagley's scholarship at Columbia, at least, Castro Faria may have mixed up the dates. He may have been thinking of the fund intended to support anthropological research, which was only established after Quain's death, according to his instructions. As for the luxury restaurant, curiously enough, I would discover much later a reference to another dinner, also in a Copacabana restaurant, this time with the anthropologist Alfred Métraux. The two anecdotes revealed a dimension of Quain's personality that no person and no document I had seen dared to mention directly.

Some tried to use his fantasies to explain his death. At the end of 1938, writing to announce Charles Wagley's arrival in Rio, William Lipkind wrote to Heloísa: 'He's a great kid. Don't let him chase rainbows like Buell.' Lipkind was referring to his colleague's frustrated expedition to the Trumai of the Coliseu River. Five years later, on 30 April 1943, Heloísa herself was forced to reply to the preposterous indignation of one John J. Feller of St Louis, Missouri. Her reply gives an idea of how far mythologizing can go.

Dear Sir,

I'm sorry to disappoint you, but the information you have received about Dr Buell Quain's search for a legendary City of Gold is entirely groundless and not supported by the slightest conceivable evidence.

Buell Quain was an anthropologist who carried out his field work among certain tribes along the tributaries of the Xingu River, in the state of Mato Grosso. His field notes and observations are of strictly scientific interest and contain no references to wanderings in search of gold or lost cities. Their only use is scientific. His second expedition to Brazil took him to the Krahô Indians, who live in the south of the Maranhão. Dr Quain first arrived in Brazil in 1938. There is therefore no basis for your claim that he had undertaken an expedition in 1927.

'I can imagine that he fantasized about a world without rich people, because that was really an ideology with him. He did not want to come over as rich. It was his most striking trait. I have no doubt about that. It was so strange, inviting me to a fancy restaurant in Copacabana while he lived in a dump in Lapa. There was this tension between his public and his private life, because he absolutely refused to live quietly like a rich man. But he made that possible for his friends. He was obsessed with not appearing to be what he really was. He tried to shelter his private life from any outside contact,' Castro Faria told me.

At the end of April 1938, Castro Faria embarked from Corumbá on the *Eolo*. The little boat would take him up the River Paraguay to Cuiabá and his meeting with Lévi-Strauss. On the boat, he was surprised to glimpse, under the bed of a cabin whose door had been left open, a book called *Unter den Naturvölkern Zentral-Brasiliens* by the German ethnologist Von den Steinen. This told the story of an expedition to the Upper Xingu in the second half of the nineteenth century. It had never been translated into Portuguese, though it was considered both a precursor and a classic of Brazilian ethnography. The passenger in that cabin could only be in the same field. 'I met him on board a boat that was going from Corumbá to Cuiabá. I made a note in my diary: "Ethnologist on board."' Buell Quain was travelling from Porto Esperança to Cuiabá, and from there he planned to proceed to the Trumai. To Castro Faria's shock, Quain, once they arrived, helped unload a truck of Lévi-Strauss's baggage. The gesture reinforced Castro Faria's notion that Buell Quain 'took great pains to show that he was nobody, as if he were a servant'.

Because I kept prodding into Quain's personal life, Castro Faria ended up admitting that he had, indeed, heard of the young American's eccentricities. But he repeated that, as far as he knew, all they signified was that he was a rich man trying to avoid being so identified. I absolutely wanted to know if Quain was married. The idea had only been suggested once that I was aware of, in his request for authorization from the Supervisory Committee. I felt it was a crucial point, so I was looking for any plausible confirmation or denial. I asked Castro Faria if it could have been a ploy the ethnologist or the National Museum might have used to get the authorization, foreseeing the problems he did indeed experience during his expedition to the

Trumai. 'During Rondon's day, there was all that ideology about not touching the Indians, not having sexual relations with the Indians, being prepared to die if necessary but never to kill. The Indian Protection Service made many mistakes in that respect. The fact that he was a foreigner must have meant a lot to them. It might have been that the IPS ideology, which was foolishly purist, thought it would be better if he were married. Boas's students were advised to bring their wives, because certain areas of indigenous culture were not open to men. You needed to have a woman to talk to the Indian women about things that remained out of sight of men. If he had really been married, I think he would have brought his wife along,' Castro Faria concluded. But I wasn't quite convinced.

I don't know if it was because I kept insisting, but eventually the elderly professor took up the theme again, without further prompting. Now, however, it was to mention Quain's 'instability' for the first time. 'As far as I know, he wasn't married. Maybe he was. Listen, he was an upper-middle-class American. He might have been married and later divorced. Besides, I always heard his parents were divorced, which might have explained his instability. It seems they drank a lot. You couldn't tell if he was really unstable. He did have that reputation, though. In Cuiabá, the first thing he did was look for a piano, which wasn't easy, and I think he did end up finding one. But Cuiabá was the end of the world. I've heard that he was a virtuoso, a musicologist. From what I've heard, the book he wrote on Fiji deals with music and dance, the field where he was most comfortable.

He was a pianist. Wherever he went, he immediately looked for a piano. And that's what he did in Cuiabá.' I imagined him running from house to house looking for a piano in the stultifying heat of that dead city, lost in the heart of Brazil. When I told the anthropologist the story, she exclaimed that it was something out of a movie, perhaps envisioning some *Fitzcarraldo*-like production.

'We spent a bit of time together in Cuiabá. Then we lost touch. Our lives took us in different directions. He was going to central Brazil, and we were crossing Mato Grosso to the Amazon,' Castro Faria continued. I asked him if Lévi-Strauss and Buell Quain had met or even perhaps got to know each other in Cuiabá. After all, they were both anthropologists and foreigners in a strange country, and I supposed that that might have brought them together. He laughed. 'No. That was very difficult. We were together, I, Lévi-Strauss, and Quain, but only on social occasions. And Lévi-Strauss didn't need anybody's company. You have to understand, he is French, a *normalien*, a Frenchman with a philosophical background. He's withdrawn, the way philosophers often are. As though they're different, always pondering complex matters. That's probably the reason Lévi fell off his mule. He made a mistake that nobody with experience of travel and field work would ever commit: he fired a gun while riding the mule. So he ended up lost and without his mule. He's a very silent person. Whenever I met Quain, our conversations were very formal, and Heloísa Alberto Torres was the boss. He always seemed friendly to me. But there was a certain reserve.'

Nevertheless, it seemed unlikely to me that, despite what Castro Faria said, Lévi-Strauss and Buell Quain hadn't established some sort of connection on that occasion. They were staying in the same hotel, the Esplanada, which belonged to a Lebanese. They were both preparing for their expeditions. What actually happened, as I later learned, is that they actually hit it off immediately. In his report on the Krahô Indians a year later, Quain affirmed his views had been influenced 'by my contact with Lévi-Strauss'. They spent entire nights in conversation, in Cuiabá, which explains why the young American sought out the French anthropologist, when he most needed to unload. He was very disturbed on that occasion. To judge by certain symptoms on his skin, he thought he had caught syphilis from a casual encounter with a girl he'd met during Carnival in Rio. He said that he'd trusted the girl because she said she was a nurse. Lévi-Strauss advised him to go back to Rio to confirm the diagnosis and get treatment, but Quain didn't listen. Years later, in New York, the French anthropologist reported their meeting to Ruth Benedict.

After much delay, mostly the result of an ear infection, Quain left Cuiabá on 17 June, en route to the Xingu and the Trumai. On the night before he left, he wrote to Heloísa, announcing his departure: 'You will hear from me before the rains come.'

Almost a year after meeting Lévi-Strauss in Cuiabá, Quain was waiting for the arrival of his mules in Carolina. Before departing for the village with a group of Krahô Indians, he described to Ruth Landes, rather oddly, his first impressions of his travelling companions:

> The father of the chief of the village I'm going to was a runaway slave. All the visible teeth in his upper jaw are filed on both sides. This kind of tooth-shaving that you had mentioned as a characteristic of blacks (the grinding of the inner sides of the upper incisors) is also a common symptom of congenital syphilis; they're known as 'Hutchinson's teeth'. You occasionally come across a case among the Brazilians. I've already come across three since I arrived in Brazil. I didn't think of it when we were discussing Negro traits. I should have paid more attention. Or were the outer sides of the incisors ground down?

Landes was a Jewish girl from New York who, after spending time among the blacks of Harlem, decided to study anthropology and came to Brazil to research Candomblé in Bahia. She had presumably become interested in black racial traits. The strange thing is Quain's somewhat anxious association between these traits and the symptoms of a specific pathological condition. It is also odd that he recognizes them in everyday life, and that he regrets not having paid more attention to them. It almost seems that he thought that such knowledge could help him protect himself from something, or to avoid it.

'I never heard anything of his sexual behaviour,' said Castro Faria. 'People talked after the suicide, saying all sorts of things, including that he had leprosy. There's no proof of anything. When the news of his suicide arrived – and that kind of news always causes a stir – people thought it might have been some illness. It was so unexpected. He once told me: "Castro Faria, there's nothing left for me to see in the world." He'd been a seafarer, doing the grimiest, lowliest work of all, on a boat sailing around the world. He said that he'd seen the whole world, that there was nothing left for him to see. He was a loner. Very reserved. Someone who says they've already seen the world is really someone who doesn't have any further interest in the present. You couldn't really socialize with him. I don't think he ever learned Portuguese, and he wasn't particularly interested in Brazil. Moreover, I never saw his books. I'll repeat what he said to me: "Castro Faria, I don't have anything left to do in this world. I've already seen it all." Out of the blue. Nobody could have expected that an American anthropologist, from the very best school, working in Brazil, would kill himself here. So young, yet already established. He was well known as one of Franz Boas's leading students, and Boas had great respect for him. Heloísa was especially deferential to all of Boas's students who came to Brazil.'

6

This is for when you get here and start to fear searching further, though by that point you'll have already gone too far. He must have told you about the ports he visited, the things he'd seen, always pushing off, across the world, an endless, circular search, and about the things he brought home, not the objects that haunted his mother after his death but whatever it was that got stuck in his eyes, leaving him with the expression he vainly tried to hide and which I glimpsed, through his distraction and fatigue, when he arrived in Carolina. Those eyes carried the things he had seen in the world, the death of a thief under the lash in a city of Arabia, the terror of a boy operated on by his own father, the surrender of people who begged for him to take them along with him, wherever he was going, as if he could grant them salvation. He said that no one can imagine the sadness and horror of being seen as a saviour by people who prefer to hand themselves over to the first person that comes along, even a predator, rather than remain where they are. I imagined it. I still wonder when exactly he understood that he was lost, that others might see a saviour in him, when he understood that everything could get even worse and that there were people even more degraded than he was. Because that might have been the moment when he decided to descend even further, ever deeper, even if only to lend them a hand. And when he needed me to lend him a hand, he was already beyond my reach. I think about how peculiar personalities are created. If they are like other people's, if they are like us. What could have happened to a man in his childhood to have been scarred that deeply? What sort of suffering had placed him in harmony with a world worse than his own?

7

Foreigners had to tread carefully in the Brazil of the Estado Novo. One gets the impression that they were under permanent surveillance. Of the young Columbia anthropologists who worked in the country at the end of the thirties, Ruth Landes was probably the one who felt the horror of the climate most deeply. She was both personally and professionally acquainted with persecuted intellectuals in Bahia, who had been imprisoned and intimidated by the regime, accused of being Communists. They helped her with access to the Candomblé rituals, the subject of her research. Her correspondence with Ruth Benedict is revealing. In a letter from May 1938, Landes mentions having received 'sad news' from Quain – that he was stuck in Cuiabá with an ear infection. She reported that he would give Benedict more details in a letter that he would send via Bolivia, for security reasons. Landes apologizes for her 'somewhat awkward' language, explaining that for reasons of security she too must write obscurely. Quain was also exhausted by the difficulties he faced in reaching the Xingu without the necessary authorizations. His solitary expedition to the Trumai ended with an explicit demand that he return to Rio de Janeiro, in the following terms: 'In accordance with the recommendation of Lieutenant-Colonel Vicente de Paulo Teixeira da Fonseca Vasconcelos, Director of the

Indian Protection Service, I hereby invite you to retire from the Trumai village where you are currently located, since your presence there constitutes an infraction of the rules and regulations of that Service. Health and fraternity, Álvaro Duarte Monteiro, Acting Regional Inspector, Ministry of Labour.' In a letter to Ruth Benedict, Heloísa Alberto Torres explains: 'Certain mistakes on the part of Mr Quain were interpreted by the Service as infractions of the law and led this institution to impose strict conditions for his continuing his research in the native villages.' Castro Faria observed that this was standard practice: 'Even I, who was the delegate-member from the Supervisory Council for Lévi-Strauss's expedition, needed a safe-conduct pass.'

In her letter of March 1939 to Ruth Benedict, Landes said that she had been 'in a state of absolute emotional solitude' after 'two weeks of horror'. She mentions a previous letter in which she had told her adviser the 'story of espionage in Bahia'. 'If you didn't receive it, it must have got "lost in the mails," more or less deliberately.'

On the eve of the war, a strong anti-American sentiment was also in the air. The young Columbia anthropologists, already wary, already susceptible to the regime's pressures, felt even more pinched, unprotected, and alone. Landes reports that in Rio, the pressure and the fear had got so acute that 'the three of us (Buell, Chuck, and I) had to accompany Dona Heloísa to the police station to get some kind of identification card for the boys'.

If Buell Quain already had something to hide, the political situation would only have given him more reason to dissemble and maintain his privacy, almost to the point of paranoia. In the letter he sent Ruth Landes on the morning he was preparing to leave Carolina, he advised her not to trust anything:

> I'm worried about your relations with Dona Heloísa. You're probably going to say that I should mind my own business. But I think that you should return her favors by being very modest around her, avoiding statements that could sound like criticism of Brazil, feigning interest in the work of Brazilian academics, and even letting her think that she is directing your research here. Of course, you could go to Rio de Janeiro and do your business without reporting to anyone. But once Dona Heloísa knows you, she is going to continue to behave strangely toward you. And if you ever have any more problems, she could be helpful. She really does have a lot of influence. There is a lot of anti-American feeling here. People scoff at Roosevelt's Good Neighbor Policy. An intellectual that Dona Heloísa suggested I meet writes pamphlets. One of them includes statements like: 'If Germany invades Brazil, the United States will defend us, but nobody can protect us from American imperialism.' It's very hard for me to refute such things in Portuguese. Normally, I just play dumb and leave it at that.

I asked Castro Faria about the impact of the young American ethnologist's suicide amidst this state of things.

'I don't think his suicide had any national impact. I don't even know what the local reactions were. A death in the interior is very different from something that happens here. It was completely unforeseen, despite his eccentricities, which people noted. Especially the thing about money, trying to conceal the possibility that he could solve all economic problems with his and his family's money. The suicide didn't traumatize any of us. It was a surprise. Quain was an aberration in the history of anthropology and in the relationship between Columbia and the National Museum. But the relationship continued without a hitch.'

Strained relations with the American anthropologists intensified in the case of William Lipkind. Dona Heloísa openly preferred Quain and Wagler. 'They are more polite, better-looking, and more charming,' Ruth Landes explained in a letter to Ruth Benedict. To complete the tableau, Lipkind had a big ego. He even haggled with Dona Heloísa over the price of the ethnographic materials he had brought back from the villages with her help, and that, unsurprisingly, greatly irritated her. 'It was said that William Lipkind had also got mixed up in other things, because he wrote political reports for the Americans. That's only hearsay, but it seems that in one of the reports he wrote about the Karajá he mentioned the information he needed to send to the State Department. It seems that he – along with many other Americans – was here as an observer,' said Castro Faria.

8

This is for when you get here. If you really do want to know. When we left the party, I went ahead and invited Dr Buell to stop by my house. He barely recognized me. I asked him if he was concerned about the next day's departure. He tried to decline my invitation. I kept insisting. He finally accepted out of politeness, because he didn't know how things were done here, because he didn't know who I was. He was tired. We drank and talked. We needed to get to know each other. It was the first night. I asked if it was his first visit to a village. He laughed. It was like a provocation. He was offended and didn't stop talking. He talked about the Trumai, and I imagined them. Everything he said from that point on I tried to imagine. Now that I think about it, I realize that it was only nine nights. But it felt like a lifetime. The first, the night before he left for the village. Then seven more when he came through Carolina in May and June, when he came to my house in search of shelter. And the last when I accompanied him on the first part of his journey back to the village. We slept in the forest, beneath a starry sky. I volunteered for the last night. He hadn't requested my company, but I felt I needed to go, even if it was only for part of the way. I may somehow have sensed something I couldn't really have known, which was that I would never see him again. What I'm telling you now is a combination of what he told me and of what

I imagined during those nine nights. How I imagined his dream and his nightmare. Heaven and hell. On the first night, he spoke to me of an island in the Pacific, where the Indians are black. He spoke of the time he had spent among those Indians and of a village, which he called Nakoroka, where everyone decides what they want to be. You can choose your sister, your cousin, your family, and your caste, every aspect of your relationship to other people. A very rigid society. But every individual can choose his own role. In that village, an outsider could never identify family traits or blood families, since all relatives, like all identities, are elective. Heaven: a dream for a boy anthropologist. He wanted to study zoology, but all it took was one term in college to set him along another road. I don't know how well you knew him. Do I have to remind you of what happened in March 1931, after he passed his mid-term exams? To celebrate, he and a few friends got on a bus to Chicago, where they drank themselves silly and went to the movies. It was the last thing he expected, like a message from the Lord. And even the night he told me about it, he still wasn't sure how much had been the effect of drink. In the darkness of the cinema the silver light burst upon the screen and a life he had never known was laid out before him, a new possibility, an exit, like an unexplored road suddenly opening before him. He didn't have any idea what film he was about to see when he came into the cinema, just as he had no idea what destiny would be revealed to him there. He sat transfixed by a love story set in the South Pacific. About a love the native society prohibited. A love condemned by the gods. A taboo. Until the night when he told me of it, he didn't know how much that forbidden love had influenced his own vocation. When he left the cinema he could only recall the bodies of the natives outlined by the sun and the water, like drops of silver, like pearls, glistening on the bodies, reflecting the sun against the sky. He would go and find them. He left the picture house determined. His friends hadn't seen what he did. The world had become different. The world was no longer there, where he was. It was somewhere else. It's important to understand that everyone sees things that nobody else can see. And that their reasons lie within these things. Everyone sees his own mirages. He dropped out of college and set sail, as a ship's apprentice, for Shanghai. He spent six months abroad. It was hard. He came back as a 'seaman first class'. He wanted to see the islands of the South Pacific, the enchanted isle of a film, the drops of silver of a forbidden love. I don't know how well you knew him. Much better than I did, I'm sure. But would it be too much for me to say that Dr Buell, my friend, drank with me and told me what he was looking for among the Indians? He wanted to discover laws that revealed how foolish ours were. And he wanted to find a place where he would finally fit in. A world that could take him in? The drop of silver of a taboo. In Shanghai he met a Chinese boy who wanted to leave China for good. Dr Buell spoke of America as if it were a dream. And, in his naiveté, he thought that he could help the Chinese achieve his dream, just as he had decided to pursue his own. He made promises he couldn't keep. One person's dream is another person's reality. The same can be said of nightmares. He managed to help the boy stow away *on the ship. But he couldn't help him reach America. He was discovered, expelled, and punished before the horrified eyes of his young American benefactor. He couldn't rule out the possibility that the Chinese boy had been killed, for having mingled with the whites. Dreams are a point of view. A viewpoint. But no matter how much he talked to me about Fiji and Vanua Levu, his island in the South Pacific, I couldn't manage to see it. It was as if the ten months he had spent there were nothing more than a dream. What he told me blew away, like clouds. And I couldn't imagine it. I couldn't conceive of the village he lived in, since it was on an island, not by the sea but in the interior, along the path to the mountains. The eyes cannot see. When he showed young island natives Western magazines with photographs that the older people could not even have understood, he always asked them if the people shown were men or women. To help me see it, when he came back to Carolina in May, he brought a photograph and a drawing he had made himself. They were portraits of two strong Negroes, who posed for him with bare torsos and distant expressions in their eyes.*

I might not have been able to imagine heaven, but hell I could see. A nightmare is a way to face fear with the eyes of a person dreaming. When he spoke of the Trumai, I heard him speak of fear. He spent four months among them, between August and November 1938. Until he was called back to Rio, in December. He went from Cuiabá to Simões Lopes in a lorry, and then spent another six days travelling through the forest on muleback. Then there was another week in three canoes down the Coliseu until he found the mission maintained by an American couple, the Reverend Thomas Young and his wife, whose names I recognized among the letters he left when he killed himself. Two white men and a boy helped him with the canoes. Dr Buell rowed one of them. At the end of the second day, at nightfall, one of the canoes started leaking and they had to stop to dry the wet baggage on a rock. It was only the following morning that they realized that the sun hardly reached the rock. They were in the middle of the rainforest. But despite the wind, they didn't meet real gusts until the fifth day. One of the canoes crashed into a rock, and the provisions were thrown overboard.

9

In a letter dated 1 November 1940, Quain's mother told
Heloísa Alberto Torres about the missionaries of the River
Coliseu. Without quinine, and with men dying of malaria,
the Americans began to pray. 'That is when they saw a man
with a shaved head, ragged trousers, and an old jacket
coming out of the river toward them. They thought he was
an escaped prisoner, until he smiled at them.' In their
delirious nightmare, they must have seen a condemned
man with chains on his hands and feet, struggling through
some swamp in Louisiana or Mississippi. Or at least that's
how I imagined the feverish, frightened visions of the poor
missionaries when I read the letter. According to his mother,
Quain had given them different medicine, which miracu-
lously tore them from their delirium. For these people, the
recovery made him into a kind of saviour, an answer to the
prayers and faith of desperate people. By chance, Quain's
mother had read an article about the treatment in a medical
journal and sent the clipping to Rio de Janeiro. And the
medicine had saved their lives. Though she was far away,
Fannie tried to make herself useful in whatever way she
could, accompanying her son on his descent into hell. At
the end of 1940, still tormented by Buell's death and
persisting in her search for answers, Fannie Dunn Quain
went to Chicago to hear a talk given by the missionaries

Thomas and Betty Young at the Moody Institute. The talk was illustrated with pictures Buell had taken among the Trumai. I imagine that when she went up and introduced herself, congratulating them, she didn't ask them any questions. Partly, perhaps, because it would have been awkward, but partly because she feared they would reveal something she didn't want to hear. It is also possible that when she died ten years later she had still not managed to ask anyone anything. She preferred to believe that nobody else knew anything she herself didn't know. After her son's death, she asked Dona Heloísa more than once if she could help the Indians, help them with the money Buell had left. Her tormented insistence leaves the impression that she was trying subconsciously, under a veil of philanthropy, to buy the silence of the Indians – or to bribe her own conscience.

Quain spent three weeks with the missionaries before continuing on down the river, through the territory of hostile tribes, until he reached the village. The Trumai who went with him sang at night and stopped speaking at sunrise. The climate of animosity and terror among the several tribes in the region forced them to light bonfires, announcing their presence, as soon as they entered 'foreign' territory. They wanted to go to every length to avoid surprises and unexpected encounters, hoping to avoid tragic incidents and misunderstandings. As they travelled down the Coliseu, the mere sight of a Kamayurá canoe gave cause for concern. Quain reached the Trumai village in the middle of August. The region was extremely inaccessible and isolated, on the banks of the Culuene river, at the point where it met the Coliseu. Waterfalls obstruct access to the region via the Xingu river. Once feared for their numbers and their courage in warfare, the Trumai had been reduced to a single village of four huts, with a fifth under construction. There were seventeen men, sixteen women, and ten children. They had settled in that place two years before, mainly because they were fearful, nervous, and wanted to escape their tribal enemies, especially the Kayabi and the Nahukwá, whose chief was a powerful shaman. The Suyá had expelled their ancestors from the same region. But now the Trumai were mainly afraid of the Kamayurá, their closest neighbours, who in the past had carried off all the girls in the village and were now trying to frighten Quain as well, saying that the powerful shaman, the chief of the Nahukwá, would come for him. In fact, when they finally met, the Kamayurá chief treated Quain with disdain and apparent indifference. He was essentially resentful that the anthropologist had chosen to stay with the contemptible Trumai rather than in the Kamayurá village. The Kamayurá invented stories and legends to intensify the feeling of terror. They had a sharply developed feel for psychological evil. And they must somehow have perceived the psychic vulnerability of the anthropologist, so much so that they played on his loneliness and delicate mental balance, saying that his father was coming in a plane with numerous gifts for the Trumai, or that a plane full of whites had just landed at Thomas Young's mission on the Coliseu river. And then the Trumai themselves intensified the hysteria with their own stories. They accused the Kamayurá of, among other things, torturing their prisoners and eating their brains. 'The Trumai continually expect the Suyá and the Kamayurá to attack at night. All it takes to get the men to race, trembling, into the middle of the village with their bows and arrows, is for a branch to break after nightfall,' Quain wrote to Ruth Benedict.

I twice interviewed Lévi-Strauss in Paris, long before I knew that I would one day become interested in the life and death of an American anthropologist he had met during his brief stay in Cuiabá in 1938. Long before I had ever heard of Buell Quain. In one of the interviews, he referred to a controversy about French racism and xenophobia. His position had been misinterpreted, so he restated his argument: 'The more cultures communicate with each other, the more they tend to become uniform, the less they have to communicate. The problem for humanity is to make sure there is enough communication between cultures, but not too much. When I was in Brazil, more than fifty years ago, I was profoundly moved, of course, by the plight of those little cultures, threatened with extinction. Fifty years later, I am surprised to note that my own culture is threatened too.' Every culture, he said, tries to defend its identity and individuality by resisting and opposing other cultures, and it was time to defend the threatened individuality of his own culture. He was speaking of the threat of Islam, but he could just as well have been talking of America and Anglo-Saxon cultural imperialism.

The greatest threat to the Trumai while Quain was visiting them was not the whites. They could no longer defend themselves against the other Indians. They were endangered. Despite their fears, most contact between the regional tribes was friendly, though it was punctuated by the visitors' occasional thefts and threats. This was especially serious when the hosts were the weakened Trumai, because they couldn't respond. The Trumai always tried to get on the good side of their visitors, even those who threatened and despised them, like the Kamayurá. They signed their first treaty with the whites in 1884. During an expedition to central Brazil, the other tribes warned Von den Steinen about the dangerous Trumai of the Upper Xingu, who were then considered bellicose towards all foreigners, since they were always at war with their neighbours. But just like the pioneering German explorer, Quain had a different experience. After the initial contact, the withered but fearsome Trumai received both with great amity. This hospitality, in fact, was inspired more by their dread of their neighbours than by any formal code of etiquette. At first, the young Columbia ethnologist had a hard time living among them. They called him Captain. Upon his arrival, he shaved his head and his eyebrows. This perplexed his hosts, since that was a Suyá custom. Then they stole all his clothes, which were coveted as protection against mosquitoes. He then had to improvise some outfits from his mosquito netting. He hardly spoke the language, and he didn't understand the family relations and the social organization of the village.

(Alongside the nuclear family, the Indians had also established symbolic family relations, which helped organize
the society, codifying its taboos and defining the duty of
each individual. The laws and the logic of these societies
were expressed in these 'classificatory relations'. The main
object of this extremely complex code was to avoid incest
in predominantly endogamous communities, which sometimes counted no more than a few dozen members.)
When Quain tried to talk to the Indians, before he knew
exactly how to behave or what to do, they asked him to
sing the songs with which he had initially entertained
them. 'They refuse to tell me their terms for these relationships – which prevents me from understanding how
they regulate incest,' he reported in a letter to Benedict.
Only much later, in my conversations with the Krahô
about the anthropologist, did I connect this phrase to my
other suspicions, which may or may not have been well-
founded.

At first Quain found the Trumai 'annoying and dirty'
('These people are wearisome and don't know it'), in
contrast to the natives he had lived with in Fiji, who now
seemed models of dignity and reserve. He contrasted the
Trumai to his only other experience in the field:

> They sleep around eleven hours a night (a sleep
> tormented by fear) and two hours during the day. They
> don't have anything better to do than to watch me. A
> child of eight or nine already seems to know everything
> he needs to know about life. The demands of the adults

are relentless. I don't like them. There is no ceremony to physical contact, and so I come over as unfriendly for trying to avoid being touched. I don't like being smeared with body paint. If the people were nicer-looking, I wouldn't mind as much, but they are the ugliest people in the whole Coliseu.

The ethnologist compared the shrivelled-up Trumai to the muscular men of Fiji, whom he had portrayed in his drawings and photographs. In the same letter to Benedict, he says: 'My illness is a particular source of anguish and insecurity over my future,' without specifying what illness he means.

Two and a half months later, he was integrated. And so he allowed himself to refuse the Indians' requests, for example when he was depressed and they wanted him to sing. Physical violence was not permitted in the village, especially against children, and Quain twice almost set off an uproar when he slapped the hand of a boy who was stealing his flour and accidentally stepped on another boy's foot. Conflicts, generally connected to matters of sex and adultery, were either substituted by magical practices or were worked through in cathartic representations. In these, the parties concerned unloaded their emotional differences through symbolic actions in a kind of improvised theatre at the heart of the village. Every once in a while the ethnologist observed the younger Indians embracing each other, or playing sexual games. To keep the Indians from lying in his hammock, he told everyone who asked that his 'wife would be angry' if she knew. There were no virgins in the village. To discourage the women who visited him, he threatened to rape them, at which they immediately ran off, usually laughing heartily. He was entirely alone.

10

This is for when you get here. All he could do was observe. Theoretically, that was the only reason he was there, among the Trumai. When he got here, he was tired of being an observer. But he was also horrified at the idea of getting mixed up in the cultures he was observing. He told me that for the natives he had lived with on his Melanesian island, there was no greater shame for a boy than to be accused of spying on women. It was a sign of childishness. They believed that peeping Toms were incapable of achieving sexual satisfaction by normal means. He was tired of observing, but nothing could have repulsed him more than living like the Indians, eating their food, participating in their daily lives and their rituals, having to pretend to be one of them. He tried to keep his distance and therefore, in a vicious circle, ended up as even more of an observer. The Trumai children, he mentioned, were exceptions. He tried to get closer to them in order to understand their games. Perhaps by some strange affinity, because of the uncomfortable space he himself occupied in the village, he immediately made note of an orphan among them. He was about ten or twelve years old, and was kept at the fringe of village life. He didn't fit in. The only one there who, like Quain himself, had no family. Since there were no teenage girls, the sexual games occurred between the boys or between boys and men, almost always initiated by the former, whom the adults did not reject. He observed that the orphan paid special attention to these games. He sought out older men, who didn't turn him away. I don't know if the boy sought him out as well, and whether that's the reason he told me the story. Another boy, immediately after his first erection, appeared one night at Dr Buell's house to boast about it, and at another point managed to copulate with a girl, deliberately, knowing the anthropologist was watching, to show off. Sex made my friend feel even lonelier. He also seems to have been impressed, so much so that he told me this on that first night, after the party in Carolina, that Trumai boys, when they were undergoing their initiation rites for the passage into adulthood, were abraded over their entire bodies with a sharp armadillo foot. It was a test of courage, a reward and an honour – though many, frightened and horrified, covered in blood, cried out in pain during the sacrifice. The Trumai greatly admired scars. The seven-year-old boys proudly showed off the marks that ceremonies had left on their bodies, he said. And then, to my surprise, he opened his own shirt and showed me a scar running from his abdomen to his chest. He smiled, waiting for my reaction. I didn't know what to say. Perhaps disappointed with my stunned expression, or possibly awoken by my shock, which brought him back after a lapse of consciousness, he re-buttoned his shirt. He mentioned laconically that he had been operated on in childhood and then that it was late, he needed to go. He never brought up the subject again. All this on that first evening, when we didn't even know

*each other. And today, as I remember Dr Buell's words, all
that comes to mind is the image of his hanged corpse, sliced
with a razor on his neck and arms, covered with blood,
dangling above a puddle of blood. That was how the Indians
found him, and how they described the scene upon arriving
at my house. I still remember his perplexed remark that the
Trumai, though they were dying out, still performed abor-
tions and killed newborns. He thought they were, perhaps
unknowingly, committing a kind of collective suicide, a
collective self-destruction. Unlike the other tribes, they had
no contact with the whites. They didn't know of anything
beyond the Coliseu and Culuene rivers. They had under-
gone no process of acculturation, though, defeated by the
Kamayurá, they had subsequently absorbed parts of their
masters' culture. Besides this collective-unconscious form of
suicide, he said, he witnessed no case of actual suicide
during his time among the Trumai. The odd thing is that
when he was forced to interrupt his work, he had forgotten
to ask them whether there had ever been a suicide among
them. Nevertheless, he still thought they had suicidal
temperaments. 'The important thing,' he told me on that
first night in Carolina, when I couldn't make sense of what
he was really talking about, 'is that the Trumai see death
as an escape and a liberation from their fears and suffer-
ings.' Once he fell sick and one of his Indian friends offered
to stab him, to free him from the pain. Their infanticides
were not just random. Birth was worse. He said: 'A culture
is dying.' Now, when I think of his words, full of enthusiasm and sadness, it seems to me that he had found a*

people whose culture was the collective representation of an aspect of his own personality. And I understand why he so longed to return to the Trumai, to the hell he described. As if a kind of stubbornness had blinded him. He wanted to keep them from disappearing for ever. The book he would write about them would become a way of keeping them alive – and of keeping himself alive.

When he spoke of the Indians' courage, I understood fear. He said courage and I heard fear. Two weeks after he arrived in the Trumai village, he witnessed a healing cere-mony. The chief's wife was sick and no remedy had been able to help her. The Indians decided to carry out the ritual. The men shut themselves into one of the houses, around the sick woman. The ritual was prohibited to women. When Dr Buell tried to enter, the chief's sister told him that he, like the women, would die if he set foot there. He ignored her and went in anyway. There was another time when they spoke to him about death, though they allowed him to draw his own conclusions. Once, when they were hunting birds for their decorative feathers, they told him that a red-headed bird they called 'lê' was an augur of death for whoever saw it. Shortly thereafter he came across the fateful apparition and chose to believe that they were playing a joke on him. He didn't say anything, though he was quite disturbed by it, so much so that he dreamed more than once of the bird appearing before him. He awoke, panting, in a sweat. He asked me what I thought about those dreams. And before I could reply, he said that the Trumai considered dreams a way of seeing while asleep.

It was common for children to wake up sobbing in the middle of the night. Their dreams were provoked by their parents' fears of enemy attack. One night, during his first month there, he awoke to the sound of women screaming. Everyone was running, with their children and their hammocks, to one side of the village. He thought they were being attacked by another tribe. During the panicked run, someone told him – or at least that is what he understood – that a woman had been shot. When the dust settled, he found out that she had been startled by a lump of clay. The women had even more reason to fear attack than the men. They knew that capturing them was one of the primary objects of warfare. The Trumai lived in a permanent state of terror. I told Dr Buell that some Indians customarily throw stones when they approach farmhouses, perhaps a means of expressing friendship. He told me that they might really have been visited that night by the Suyá, who were feared for their unrivalled ferocity. According to the Trumai, the sun created all the tribes, except for the Suyá, who were descended from cobras. The entire Trumai village wanted to sleep in the little house they had built in one week for Dr Buell, because he had a pistol. Every once in a while they would ask him to fire into the darkness that surrounded the village, to frighten off their enemies. Even if the Suyá came with good intentions, the Trumai feared them too much to ever be able to regard them as friends. Mere mention of the Suyá threw the Trumai into panic. Life was insecurity, and it always got worse at night. The slightest motion in the darkness unleashed a veritable chaos.

One stormy day, dark as night, Quain, prostrated by fever, experienced the horror that tormented the Trumai. Though they did not share the strong belief in the supernatural of the Kamayurá, they feared lightning bolts and thunderclaps. They thought someone was disturbing the rains. During the first tropical downpour he witnessed in the village, Dr Buell received a breathless visit from Aloari, his assistant and cook, who came to beg him to turn out his lamp and stop working, since he was irritating the rains. It was different on that feverish day when the storm turned day into night. He saw two eyes at the door of his hut. They weren't the deep eyes of Aloari, with his large lips and his dishevelled hair cut in the shape of a gourd. They were burning eyes, loose in the void, seeming to float in the viscous matter of the darkness and the rain. And all he said was: 'The eyes of someone I knew.' For me, the nightmare was imagining the return voyage, the thirty-eight days heading up the rivers in a boat, through enemy territory, in fear of deadly arrows, and then on foot and by truck across kilometres and kilometres of dust and earth. That was what he would have to face, leaving behind that end of the world, though all he wanted to do was stay on, and though he was still annoyed by the Indian Protection Service's decision to force him to leave immediately. During his return, as he headed upriver, on 7 November 1938, an eclipse lasting somewhat over an hour made the moon disappear from the sky as soon as it came out. The Indians travelling with him said they could not go on until they had exorcised the evil that was eating the moon. First, they asked him to fire into the air. Then they danced and shot arrows into the sky. One of the Indians decided to go back, terrified of being murdered by the whites. Finally, the chief stood up and spoke at length to the moon, until it reappeared out of the emptiness.

11

On his way back to Cuiabá, Buell Quain came down with an attack of malaria. While he was recovering, he sent Ruth Benedict a narrative of his time among the Trumai: 'Every death is a murder. Nobody expects to make it through the next rainy season. Imaginary attacks are common. The men press together, terrified, in the middle of the village – the most exposed place of all – and expect to be targeted by arrows coming out of the dark forest.'

Nobody ever asked me, so I never needed to reply that hell, as I imagine it, is, or was, the Xingu of my child-hood. It is a prefabricated house, made of wood painted puke-green, built on stakes to protect the inhabitants from the animals and the nocturnal attacks to which, on the ground floor, they would be easy prey. It is a solitary house in the middle of nowhere, erected in a flat clearing in the forest, surrounded by jungle-rice and death. Everything that isn't green is grey. Or else it's earth and mud. A dirt road leads to the stairs at the entrance to the house, but that road, in the other direction, does not appear to lead to any known location. The easiest way to get there is by plane, not a large one, two engines at the most, some-thing that can land on the unsealed strip beside the house. From above, as the plane approaches with a rumble, that is all we see: the solitary house with the landing strip beside it, in a large clearing covered with high grass, surrounded on all sides by an endless forest. The dirt road leads from the house to the landing strip and then heads directly into the forest, where it disappears, like everything there, looking for a way out – or, perhaps, hinting at a tendency towards suicide. I've heard that now everything has changed and that the region is unrecognizable. The tropical rainforest has given way to the fields of huge ranches. The forest has disappeared, chopped down and burned, but in those days it asserted itself like a terrifying danger, so much so that it was hard for a child to understand for what purpose people had come to that distant wilderness. The house was at the centre of a ranch called Vitoriosas, if I'm not mistaken, because its owner, Chiquinho da Vitoriosas, as he was known in the area, owned a bus company of the same name. It was the ranch closest to the one my father had decided to establish, in 1970, in the Xingu. He christened it Santa Cecília in honour of the cousin he was living with at the time, the one who, humiliated by her own passionate excesses, would soon start hounding him with lawyers. She was trying to recover the money she had loaned him, the money he had squandered on that land, supposedly good for livestock. At the same time, he was seeing other women more or less openly. My father had to stop at Vitoriosas – in the middle of nowhere, in the middle of the forest – when he went to see how things were going with the road he was opening up in the middle of the jungle. This was meant to connect Chiquinho's territory to Santa Cecília. He would have completed it, if it hadn't been for the literal sea of mud that swallowed it up after the trees were chopped down and the panting tractors had passed, the levelling trucks of civilization.

I don't even remember what Chiquinho da Vitoriosas looked like, but I do remember his death in a plane crash. Maybe I'm only now dreaming this up. But I seem to have a recollection of my father stooped over someone, maybe the widow, telling her not to lose hope, that there was still a chance they would find the little plane that had been missing for days. Every time we visited Vitoriosas, there was a dark house, with armed men, silent, withdrawn women, and a heavy sky, lightning and black clouds. When the sun was not hidden behind a fog it called to mind an inhospitable planet from some science-fiction movie like *Lost in Space*. I also remember the sound of boots on the dusty wooden floorboards, and seeing, through the cracks, the red earth below. My father confided that Chiquinho's death was simply what careless pilots had coming. Those who flew too low, between the clouds and the forest canopy, in order to avoid the storms up in the cumulonimbus. My father flew as high as he could, relying only on his navigational instruments. Those planes weren't pressurized, so they couldn't fly above the clouds. But the problem with flying too low was that a mountain could suddenly loom out of nowhere. Any unexpected change in the terrain could cause the plane to crash into rocks and trees. My father always vaunted his caution, so much so that he had the fuselage of his Cessna 310 painted with a tortoise – which he, like the Indians, called a *tracajá* – with a bundle on its back and the motto 'Slowly but surely'. That wasn't the whole story. Once the terror of the moment was past, there were various incidents that entered family legend. Even if they don't prove that my father's aeronautical skills were limited, even if they weren't exactly displays of impetuousness, they nevertheless betray a measure of imprudence. My brother-in-law told of flying with my father. They could not see past the ends of their noses as they flew through a cumulonimbus, a 'CB', as my father referred to the purplish nightmare of those cathedrals in the sky. They were suddenly stunned by the sight of a hill straight ahead of them, a few hundred metres away. My father immediately jerked the plane upwards in a terrified vertical ascent, straight through the cloud. The two left that dark, lightning-filled world to emerge into the sunny blue sky of the higher altitudes. Only then, with his heart in his throat, did my brother-in-law see how frightened my father was, silent, trembling, thick saliva on his lips, dried at the corners of his mouth. Another episode also became notorious. My father was concerned to reach the airport in Cuiabá before six in the evening, because his pilot's licence did not permit him to fly at night. My father thought the air-traffic controller was saying that it was getting late and that he needed to hurry. All he was really saying was that one of the runways was undergoing repairs. That was the same runway my father, fearful of committing an infraction and losing his licence, was heading for. He ended up landing on a tractor in the middle of an excavated building site, where armed soldiers had been awaiting him since the plane, heading straight for the landing strip the tower had told him to avoid, turned up on the horizon. My father was arrested as soon as he set foot on the ground. The badly damaged plane was impounded. It was the beginning of the seventies, and the military feared that the airport, a secured area, was under terrorist attack.

I myself participated, as spectator and victim, in two of these episodes. The less serious occurred when my father forgot to mix the oil, a standard procedure that should have been carried out during the flight, as we spent more than an hour in a hail- and lightning-storm between São Miguel de Araguaia and Goiânia. The right-hand motor froze. He was so worked up over the situation that he didn't even see the propeller slowing down, making a toc, toc, toc sound on my side of the plane, which is why I tapped his arm, speechless, and pointed through the window. Immediately, livid, he jiggled the controls on his side and the motor started up again. There were other incidents. I must have been ten when he suffered an attack of malaria as we arrived in Barra do Garças, where he had gone to collect money from the Superintendence for the Development of Amazônia. He was shaking uncontrollably. I thought he was going to die, leaving me alone there at the end of the world. I could hardly imagine how to get away. He not only survived but even escaped another attack of malaria when he was flying alone above the jungle. I prefer not to imagine his fear and desperation.

Buell Quain had also accompanied his father on business trips. When he was fourteen, they went to a Rotary Club convention in Europe. They visited Holland, Germany, and Scandinavia. From then on, he never stopped travelling. For Quain, who had left the Midwest to head towards civilization, the exotic seemed like a kind of paradise, something different and better, something that left open the possibility of an escape from the stifling environment he had been born into. My travels with my father, to the contrary, led me to equate the exotic with hell itself. I always had to go with him to Mato Grosso and Goiás, because we were legally required to spend holidays together. My parents were separated and had reached a court agreement over my custody and support. And he needed to visit his ranches. There were two: one in the semi-forested area between the Rio das Mortes and the Rio Cristalino, in the region of Araguaia, at the latitude of São Miguel, near the Ilha do Bananal, and the other in the Xingu, in the middle of virgin rainforest. My first trip to the jungle was in 1967, when I was six and my father was still looking for land to acquire. That was the objective of the trip. There's a faded photo of me at his side outside the National Congress, in Brasília, where we stopped over before heading on to the Araguaia. My father's suit is rumpled from the journey, and I, who reach his waist, am dressed up like a cowboy for a carnival ball, with a vest and brown boots. Since 1966, he had been in Brasília negotiating the acquisition of two

ranches in the backlands, and had received two clear titles
from the government. It was an unheard-of bargain. He
not only paid a pittance for the land but in 1970 he also
began to receive subsidies for his cattle-raising project.
The practice was established under the military regime,
who, under the pretext of developing Amazônia, not only
subsidized the purchase of hundreds of thousands of acres
at bargain-basement prices, but then – nabob-style –
financed the new plantation owners' schemes. In general,
all you had to do was cut down the forest, plant grass, and
populate the land with cattle. My father must have known
the right people. The goal of the trip was to buy the land.
Originally, he planned to concentrate on the semi-forested
area. Only later, I think, did the opportunity arise in the
Xingu, a dream buy he could not resist. We stayed on the
Ilha do Bananal. At the time, my father still flew a single-
engine plane. The two of us went alone together to the
end of the world, and I kept myself busy flipping through
a first-aid and rainforest survival manual, which dealt with
the worst horrors of a forced landing or crash. There was
a description of a minuscule fish, the very thought of which
tormented me. It entered the body at the tip of the penis
and, once installed in the urethra, opened its scales or
whatever they were, so that it could never be removed.
The book was well illustrated. The landing strip on the
Ilha do Bananal was right by a Karajá village, and people
arriving there were greeted by acculturated Indians. It was
a depressing spectacle. Back then there was a hotel there
that, rumour had it, President Juscelino Kubitschek had

built for encounters with his mistresses. The landing strip was for the hotel's guests. In July 1967, the hotel had been become the setting for an exotic photo-novel in the magazine *Seventh Heaven*. It was a modern, two-storey building, reminiscent of a Brasília transplanted to the banks of the Araguaia. I've heard that it was abandoned shortly thereafter and subsequently burned down. It must be falling to pieces, if it does still exist. When we arrived, a few actors from the photo-novel were sitting at the bar next to the reception desk. With them was the Karajá chief. He was trying to convince the barman to give him another whisky. The barman refused and was mocking the chief. The actors were laughing. My father did me the favour of announcing that I was Marshal Rondon's great-grandson on my mother's side. A piece of information that, from then on, he deployed whenever he thought it necessary, like a business card, every time we went into the jungle. The revelation had an immediate effect. Before I understood what was happening, the drunken chief had already returned to the village, taken from his own son various presents he had given him (I recall an Indian club and a cockade) and was now insisting, against the wishes of the hotel manager downstairs, on coming up to our room to offer them to me as a sign of welcome.

In one of the letters he never sent to Margaret Mead, written on 4 July 1939, Quain said this:

Official treatment reduced the Indians to poverty. There is a widespread belief (among those few people

interested in the Indians) that the way to help them
is to cover them with gifts and 'raise them into civilization'. All this can be attributed to Auguste Comte,
who had an enormous influence on higher education
here and who, via his spectacular Brazilian disciple,
the aged General Rondon, corrupted the Indian
Protection Service. I still haven't been able to establish the logical connection, but I know it exists.

My father immediately hit it off with one of the
actresses, whom I would re-encounter the following
summer in Petrópolis, on a weekend when he showed up
to visit me. He came with her and her two children (their
father, the actress's ex-husband, also had a summer house
in Petrópolis). He bought me a plastic Apache fort to
console me for my disappointment with that reunion. On
the Ilha do Bananal, while the actress was being
photographed for the magazine, my father and I, with my
Jungle Jim hat and in a foul mood that was only to be
expected from a six-year-old child forced to spend days
trekking through the jungle in jeeps and motorboats
beneath a scorching sun, went off in search of the land
he was planning to buy. At the end of one afternoon, when
we arrived back on the Ilha do Bananal, the entire photo-
novel team and the family of the hotel manager were
waiting for us to cross the river to a heavenly white sandy
beach. Anyone who was hurt (or who was wearing red
shorts – so the story went) was not allowed to swim, so
as not to attract the piranhas. Even so, there were throngs

of tiny fish that bit the bathers' legs and who, the adults told me, probably to scare me, were baby piranhas. When I wasn't with my father, I played with the hotel manager's son, who must have been somewhat older than I was. During our trip, at the Leonardo Station of the Xingu Indigenous Reservation, the Villas Bôas brothers were organizing a conference of tribes that had been at war with one another for years. The Villas Bôases were trying to coax the Txikão Indians to the park, to the terror of the Waurá and the Yawalapíti, who had been living there for some time. Everyone expected an unprecedented event, a ceremony that could be presented as a spectacle for a white audience. Groups of journalists and visitors from Brazil and abroad, military authorities and invited guests, were expected at the Leonardo Station, all flown in on an air force DC-3. I don't know whose idea it was. We gatecrashed the ceremony. Or maybe the hotel manager had been invited. We left the Ilha do Bananal very early in the morning, in my father's single-engine plane, and headed towards the Xingu, flying over the forest and the Roncador Hills. The hotel manager sat up front, in the co-pilot's seat; his son and I sat in the back. As we flew over the Leonardo Station, we saw Indians pointing up at us and running towards the landing strip. The air force plane was already there. When we landed, the plane was surrounded by Indians, mostly children, who, upon seeing a boy their age, immediately began to touch me and tug off my clothes, encouraged by my fear. No matter how much I screamed and called for my father, he couldn't do anything, because he too was immobilized, surrounded by Indians. Deep down, he thought it was funny to see me taken away, most likely weary of me and my bad temper. The little Indians carried me. I felt like I was in the middle of a rushing stream. Resistance was useless. From what I could make out, they wanted to see me naked, to make me just like them. We were greeted by one of the Villas Bôas brothers – I can no longer remember if it was Orlando or Cláudio – who asked my father to sleep with me in the plane. They didn't have anywhere else to put the visitors and they feared an unexpected reaction from the Txikão, who would be arriving from elsewhere for the conference. Though both short and puny, they were greatly feared by the robust local Indians. They were considered treacherous. They attacked villages at night and carried off the bigger men's wives. The wife of one of the Txikão chiefs had been carried off while still a girl from a Waurá tribe. She returned after years of absence, married. There could be a conflict if the family decided to take her back. The news that the Txikão were approaching was enough for the big, strong Indians, painted with annatto dye, their hair cut in the shape of gourds, both Yawalapíti and Waurá, to scatter in terror. It was a grotesque scene. The scrawny little men came out of the forest, armed, and the great big Indians fled or grabbed hold of each other and hid behind the whites. That night, my father and I slept, for safety, in the plane, and the next morning I awoke in the back seat, having wet myself during the night. Terrified by the idea of the traitorous Indians and of the wildcat

that was said to be stalking the village, I didn't dare get
up in the night. I don't remember if I tried to wake my
father. When we left the next day, he had only his underwear and his watch. The Indians took the rest. They didn't
leave me with anything. I was fed up with those people.
I didn't want to give presents to anyone, even though I
departed with my hands full of the inevitable clubs, bows,
arrows, and cockades given in homage to my great-grand-
father, thanks again to my father's intervention. To bid
them farewell, my father decided at the last minute to fly
dangerously low over the Station. In my childish ignorance, I wasn't even frightened. It was like being on a
roller coaster. I wanted more, to the horror and unease
of the manager and his son. All I remember is a horde of
Indians running every which way, terrified, and the chill
in my stomach as we descended sharply towards the heart
of the Station. I can imagine the controlled fear of the
hotel manager and the irritation of the Villas Bôas brothers,
down below, forced to tolerate all sorts of hilarities and
imbecilities on the part of their guests.

An awareness of the danger only came five years later.
I was eleven. My father already had the Cessna 310, a
twin-engine. He already owned an enormous ranch,
60,000 *alqueires*, in the area to the south of the Ilha do
Bananal, on the Rio das Mortes, which he called the
Tracajá, as well as Santa Cecília, another 20,000 *alqueires*,
in the virgin rainforest, around forty kilometres from the
Rio Xingu, in the municipality of São José. Chiquinho
da Vitoriosas was not yet dead. My father was trying to

open up a road from Vitoriosas to Santa Cecília. We left
in a lorry to see how the work was coming along, taking
with us a mechanic from Goiânia who was going to try
to fix one of the tractors. We followed in the back of the
lorry that skidded through the quagmire of the sea of
mud that they called, in a display of good will, a road,
and which bounced through the middle of the jungle in
giant waves. The road ended in a clearing before a wall
of virgin forest. As we got closer, we were warned to
fasten our collars, button our shirtsleeves, and stick the
bottoms of our trouser-legs into our boots. Deforestation
had the jungle in an uproar. Animals and birds were
screaming everywhere, and swarms of black bees covered
the men's arms. My father had told me not to move, to
try not to worry about them, and hope that they didn't
get inside my shirt or trousers. All I wanted was to get
out of there. What were we doing in the middle of hell,
on a shameful, useless mission, which would be swallowed up in only a few years? The cries of the forest were
terrifying. We were waiting for the mechanic to fix the
tractor so we could return to Vitoriosas, planning to
continue to Santa Cecília by plane. At that time, the
ranch was nothing more than a small clearing surrounded
by jungle, with a few huts and a very primitive unsealed
landing strip. We spent the night in a cabin less than
three metres square, made of the trunks of small trees
poked into the beaten-earth floor, and which supported
a roof of dried leaves less than two metres high. There
were two beds – actually, two platforms made of tree

branches each raised on four stakes that had been pushed into the ground. Between the skinny tree trunks that formed the walls, snakes, scorpions, and centipedes could come and go at will. At night it was bitterly cold. My father decided to leave early the next morning. We got up before sunrise, had breakfast, and left with our baggage. It was already light when my father started the engines, but the sun was still to appear above the canopy of trees. The windshield was fogged and covered with dew. Imprudently, my father thought that the motion of the plane down the landing strip would clear the glass. That is not what happened. The mechanic was in the co-pilot's seat, and I was behind, not paying attention, reading a comic book. The plane raced down the earthen runway and suddenly began to shake to an unusual degree. My father lunged forward. I didn't notice anything at the time. The idea was that we would head toward Tracajá and thence to Goiânia, where we would drop off the mechanic and head back to São Paulo. But my father immediately announced that we would instead get off at Suiá Miçu, a gigantic ranch, an entire world, at the time owned by the Vatican, so people said, halfway between the Xingu and the Rio das Mortes. I asked my father what that cracking sound was, from the tail of the plane. He said we must have run into a bird or something and told me to keep quiet. Not another word was spoken for the duration of the journey. Only when we were approaching Suiá Miçu, when the landing strip, probably the best in the whole region, could already be seen in the distance, did my father turn to the mechanic and me and announce that he was going to turn off the engines to conserve the fuel in the tanks at the wingtips. He asked us not to worry. He recommended that the mechanic open his door before the plane touched the ground. As soon as we landed, he said, we would have to jump, because the plane could explode. I put down the comic book and focused my eyes. I still didn't know what had happened. As we left Santa Cecília, when he was trying to take off, my father had a close call. He had counted on a demisted windshield and didn't notice that he had already left the runway and entered the forest. That is when he lunged forward. He had already damaged the landing gear and was tangled amidst the trees. The wires of the radio antenna had been cut by the treetops. The noise in the tail came from the wires, thrashing in the wind. We narrowly avoided crashing into the jungle. Now, the twin-engine plane was gliding downwards, with the engines switched off and the nose pointing upwards. I was in a panic. The bottom of the plane hit the ground, since there was no landing gear. The left wing was ripped off by the impact, and we ended up with the front of the plane embedded in an earthen hut on the left side of the runway. Nobody was thrown out. Nobody was hurt. The mechanic got out. I emerged with trembling legs. Only when I was already on the ground did I start to cry and scream, in a hysterical fit, begging my father to get out of the plane. The most incredible part of it all was that, as I recall, he emerged smiling. It was a sallow smile, perhaps one of relief, perhaps to hide his fear. The ranch manager's cars immediately arrived, and after making sure nobody was hurt he invited us to lunch, gave me a tranquillizer, and told two employees to take us to a nearby village, where we could get an air taxi. We must have driven for four hours, if not more, down a dirt road, and the only plane available on the small airstrip was an ominous Bonanza, with a V-shaped tail, notorious for its instability. I have never vomited so much as I did on that trip to Goiânia, where I slept for twenty-four consecutive hours, thanks in part to the effects of the tranquillizer. When I finally got up, my father told me that they had almost called a doctor. They thought I was dying. On the day I woke up, the newspaper headlines were all about the tragedy of a Varig plane that had mysteriously crashed on its descent into Orly, killing most of the crew and all the passengers except one. The newspapers ran pictures of the dead celebrities. And I somehow associated the great tragedy with our little accident, as if there were some inexplicable connection between the two. The Xingu, in any case, was impressed upon my mind as the very image of hell. I never understood why it occurred to the Indians to move there, which seemed, if not some kind of masochism or even suicide, at the very least an incredible folly. I didn't think about the question again until August 2001, when the anthropologist who finally took me to the Krahô said to me: 'Look at the Xingu. Why are the Indians there? Because they were pushed and pursued and fled into the most inhospitable and inaccessible place, the most terrible place imaginable for their survival, and yet the only, and last, place they could survive. The Xingu was the only place left.'

I started researching the Krahô shortly after I first saw that newspaper article referring to Quain's suicide. On the morning of Sunday, 25 August 1940, a year after the ethnologist's death, the village where he had spent his final months was attacked by eleven men armed with rifles, under the command of two landowners, José Santiago and João Gomes, from the municipality of Pedro Afonso, which was then part of the state of Goiás. It was a sneaky, perversely planned ambush, a revenge meant to teach a lesson to the Indian cattle rustlers. By the time the massacre, which also targeted another village, was over, twenty-seven Indians were dead, men, women, and children. Before they attacked, the landowners offered a bull to the village of Cabeceira Grossa, knowing that the Indians would get together to share the meat. It was a trap. They attacked at dawn, as the people were unwarily eating. Taken by surprise, the Indians tried to flee into the jungle. Some went missing for days. That was the case of old Vicente, who was then still a boy and managed to flee. When I visited the Krahô, in August 2001, he told me his version of the story (he hadn't known Quain, because he was working for the whites, in Pará, during the months the American spent in the village). Women were cut down with babies at the breast. When they were attacked, the chief, Luís Balbino, made an attempt to palaver with the landowners, but he was murdered by the aggressors. They then pillaged the village, taking with them the objects Quain had left behind. Under pressure from the Estado Novo, the landowners were tried and convicted, though their sentences were probationary. The episode eventually led to the delimitation of Krahô territory and the creation of the Manoel da Nóbrega Station of the Indian Protection Service. The repercussions of the massacre were immense and can even be seen in the messianic movement that developed among the Krahô around 1952, in another village. A psychic, by all indications under the influence of marijuana, started predicting the disappearance of the whites and the transformation of the Indians into civilized people, events that were announced to him in appearances by the rain god. The movement lost credibility when the prophecies went unfulfilled.

In my search for information about the Krahô, I eventually met a couple of anthropologists who, having studied and lived among them for more than two decades, had created an independent organization to support the Indians, with both domestic and international backing. We made an appointment at the organization's headquarters in São Paulo. I told them what I was looking for and to my surprise they mentioned that they had once met an old man who was one of the two Indians who had been with Buell Quain on the night of his suicide.

During the time they lived among the Krahô, the two anthropologists had been approached more than once by the elderly João Canuto Ropkà, who asked them if they had ever heard of Dr Quain Buele, the American ethnologist whose death he had witnessed. It took them a long time to catch the name. They listened to the old man's stories without taking them very seriously, and the ignorance of these white people about one of the most traumatic and extraordinary experiences of his life both frightened and angered him. The old man could not believe that the whites didn't know who Dr Quain Buele was, the anthropologist couple told me when we met, in a room piled high with papers and files, with maps of indigenous territories spread out across the walls.

At that point, I was already completely obsessed, I couldn't think about anything else, and just like everyone else I had met, they showed no interest in my motives. Nobody asked me. I said I wanted to write a novel. In the face of my enthusiasm, which to others might have seemed crazy and inexplicable, the couple were, at first, no more than a bit standoffish. I wanted to visit the Krahô and, if possible, the site of the suicide. They listened to my story in silence, exchanging the occasional glance, which might have conveyed mistrust but perhaps was a sign of nothing more than familiarity. Perhaps they only wanted to be sure that I meant no harm to the Indians. The anthropologists told me that, by coincidence, they were planning a trip to Carolina. They had organized a meeting between representatives of several Timbira groups in the area – not only the Krahô but also the Canela and the Gavião. The husband said I could come, if I wanted to. He had promised the Krahô to bring his eldest son to the village after the meeting in Carolina. The boy, twenty-something years old, had survived an operation to correct a congenital heart defect. After putting off the medical intervention several times during his childhood and adolescence, they finally decided to have it operated on. The risky surgery was a success, and the thankful Indians, who had known the boy since his childhood, wanted to celebrate his rebirth.

By a strange coincidence, the Timbira meeting was scheduled for 31 July and 1 August so we would be going to the village on 2 August the same day that Buell Quain had committed suicide, sixty-two years before, as he attempted to travel in the other direction. The anthropologist and his son had already been in Carolina for a few days when I arrived on a flight that had stopped in Brasília, Palmas, and Araguaína. There, I was greeted by a taxi driver who did not stop talking for a single second during the entire 200-plus-kilometre trip, down an almost completely paved road, which crossed the scraggly forest covering the plateaus, beneath an inclement mid-afternoon sun.

Carolina is a dead place, as Quain observed when he first arrived there. But it has its charm, even more so today, after decades of quiet crumbling and abandonment, as if everything had stopped and been preserved in a distant age. The road from Araguaína passes right in front of the city, on the other side of the Rio Tocantins, through what is no more than a settlement, a few streets, with the extraordinary and dubious name of Filadélfia. When the river, abundant even in the dry season, appeared in front of us, and we went down to get the boat, I could see the little port on the far bank and the Pipes dock. I was immediately struck by a sinister feeling that I had seen that landscape somewhere before. It was exactly the same background I had observed in the photograph of Quain's arrival at the city, published on the front page of *O Globo* on 18 August 1939, which reported the news, somewhat tardily, of the ethnologist's suicide: 'Sensational photos of suicidal scientist in the Brazilian rainforest'.

Walking up from the port, the visitor passes the Avenida Getúlio Vargas, lined with mango trees and leading to the central church. The hotel I stayed in is only a few metres from the old single-storeyed house of Manoel Perna, which is now disfigured by tiles and aluminium siding. In Manoel Perna's house, Buell Quain found an attentive conversation partner for the nights he spent in Carolina after arriving there in March, and afterwards, during his visit to the city at the end of May and the beginning of June, when he came to pick up letters, money, and supplies, and to celebrate his birthday. And it was there that the Indians came two months later, bringing news of the tragedy and handing over to the engineer the dead man's belongings.

I barely saw the anthropologist on the day I arrived. He was much occupied with the Indians. We agreed to meet the next day, at lunchtime, outside the city, where the Krahô were gathered. He had promised to introduce me to an old man who had known Quain. I therefore had the morning free to pursue some leads relating to the death of the ethnologist, perhaps a document that may have been filed away somewhere in the city. I found nothing among the decaying records, murder trials, crimes for love and money, family feuds and suicides, stuffed into dusty boxes on forgotten shelves in windowless rooms, like anthills at the back of old houses and buildings in the middle of the back of beyond. I walked through the deserted city. It was over a hundred degrees. I ended up at the main church. The door was closed, but someone passing on a bicycle, seeing that I was trying to get in, suggested that I look for the priest in a green house on the other side of the street. I was received by a parish assistant. I asked if I could visit the church and climb the tower. I wanted to take a panoramic photograph of the city. The boy gave me the key to a side door and asked me to leave it on a nail just inside the entrance to the parish house, if by chance he wasn't home when I returned. He was about to leave for his lunch break. There was work being done to the nave, and the interior of the tower seemed unfinished, pieces of wood lying everywhere. The walls were made of brick, which had not been covered or painted, and a cement stairway rose between them, in a spiral roughly two metres in circumference. I began climbing it without a second thought. I have always been made insecure by heights, though I have never quite been phobic. As I rose, I noticed that the cement steps grew thinner and thinner. A shoddy bit of construction. I wasn't convinced that the top of the staircase could support the weight of a person. There was no handrail, and I started to grasp at the walls, sweating both from the heat and from fear. I avoided looking towards the centre of the stairwell, or down to the ground. The effort of lifting my foot to each next step increased until I realized I was crawling along the irregular cement. When I finally arrived at the top, an extraordinary landscape was spread out before me. There was the Avenida Getúlio Vargas, and the tops of its hundred-year-old mango trees, and, to my right, the Tocantins, flowing copiously through the forest towards the plateaus in the distance. Every once in a while a solitary figure appeared below, hidden in a bit of shade. I was alone. I could hear nothing besides the wind. I had never suffered from dizziness, and it seemed that now, for the first time, I realized how little control I had over my body, as if some force beyond my will could push me from the height where I stood. Somewhere to the south of all that vastness, the remains of Buell Quain were buried. I took my photos and went back down, one step at a time. I returned the key to the priest's assistant, who was still in the parish house and hadn't expected me back so soon. I didn't tell anyone about my visit to the church. At noon, as arranged, I took a taxi to the Timbira gathering, which was being held at a house eighteen kilometres outside the city, behind a sand pit to the right of the road to Imperatriz, at a place called Urupuxete. I planned to talk to old Diniz, the only living Krahô who had known Quain, when he was still a boy, and who could tell me where the ethnologist was buried. The old man didn't live in the village the anthropologist was taking me to. The gathering was the only chance I would have to talk to him.

When I arrived the Indians were having lunch. Old Diniz was seated on a long bench at the end of a large table where about twenty people were eating pasta with rice and beans. His son was at his side. He was tall, and his face bore ritual scars. He accompanied his father everywhere. The two were shirtless, wearing shorts and flip-flops. As soon as the old man finished his lunch, the anthropologist came over to introduce us. We sat to the side of the house and were soon surrounded by other Indians, who were curious and wary. At first I thought that they already knew what I wanted to discuss and were there to intimidate me, to show support for the old man, but I slowly realized that they had no idea why I was there. They were as curious as I was. They were young, they knew that something serious had happened in the remote past, something that could have bad repercussions for them, but they didn't know what it was exactly. They were surrounding him in order to both protect and control him, and to make sure he wouldn't reveal anything, if there was anything to reveal. I took my tape recorder out of my bag. That was the old man's cue to point at the machine and say: 'I've been needing one of those.' I froze. I looked at the anthropologist, helpless. I had just got there and I already didn't know how to react. 'It's the only one I've got, and I need it for my work,' I answered, following the anthropologist's advice on how to react to requests for personal property I needed for my work. I would have to give them everything else, he explained, and I did not want to seem rude or face the inconvenient possibility of being robbed. But old Diniz, noting my discomfort, was not about to give up: 'You didn't understand me. I don't want your tape recorder. I want one *just like* yours.' I tried to remain firm: 'It's the only one I've got.' The old man retorted: 'Back in São Paulo you can buy me one and mail it to me.'

The conversation had barely started and it was already going badly. The anthropologist came to my rescue. He interrupted the conversation, which otherwise could have gone on endlessly, since the old man and I both knew exactly what the other was saying and didn't want to let on that we did. To change the subject, he off-handedly asked Diniz about the 'American ethnologist', as if the idea had just popped into his mind and had nothing to do with my presence there. This beginning and my evident lack of tact left me so paralysed that I hadn't managed to turn on, or hadn't remembered to turn on, the tape recorder when old Diniz answered: 'Cãmtwỳon'. What? Hoping for a translation, I looked at the anthropologist and saw that his eyes were as taken aback as mine, affable and somewhat enthusiastic. 'That's his name!' he said, excited. 'That's what they called the American.' I asked him to repeat it. The old man repeated it, and the anthropologist wrote it down in my notebook. 'What does that mean?' I wanted to know. But nobody could be sure. The old man just repeated: 'Cãmtwỳon, Cãmtwỳon.' I spent the rest of the trip trying to find someone who could help me decipher the meaning of that name. Two days later, when I arrived at the village,

Sabino Côjam and Creuza Prumkwỳi, who of the younger generation were the most actively interested in the study of their own language, 'the village intellectuals', the anthropologist joked when he introduced me to them back in Carolina, told me that 'twỳon', meant a snail, both the land snail and its trail. The anthropologist had already told me that 'cãm' was the present, the here and now, but nobody could work out what the words meant in combination. The anthropologist explained that, contrary to what most whites believe, Indian names don't always mean anything, especially not anything to do with the personality of the person named. They belong to a repertory and are assigned at random. I would have to return to São Paulo without knowing what that name meant. But I couldn't accept that it didn't reveal anything about Quain, that there was no relationship between the name and the person. I decided for a rough, slightly moralistic explanation: 'Cãmtwỳon' became, for me, both the snail's shell and his burden in the world, the home he carries wherever he goes, his shelter, his body itself, which he can only shed in death, his here and now for ever. 'Cãmtwỳon' became, for me, the snail's trail. You cannot flee. Wherever you may go, there you will always be. The image reminded me of a remark by Francis Ponge about snails: 'Accept yourself as you are. With all your vices. In proportion to your capacity.'

'Craviro gave him the name,' the old man added.

Luís Balbino, the village chief who would be murdered in the massacre a year after Quain's death, was probably

one of the Indians who posed alongside the ethnologist
atop the wing of the Condor seaplane the day he arrived
in Carolina. He was the one who took Quain to the village.
Quain bought many things in Carolina: food, toys as presents, arms, and munitions at the shop run by the busi-
nessman and landowner Justino Medeiros Aires, one of
the 'intellectuals' Quain had mentioned in the letter he
wrote to Ruth Landes the morning he set out for the
village. As a young man, Justino had been vice-president
of the Carolina Literary Guild. He gave one of the speeches
in honour of Humberto de Campos at the ceremony Quain
attended on 8 March 1939: 'Humberto, the adolescent'.
'Justino supplied the ammunition for the massacre of the
Krahô,' Old Diniz told me. When they arrived at the village,
Balbino suggested that the anthropologist stay in the house
of Mundico until they could build him a hut. The American
spoke with Balbino and Mundico more than the others,
because they spoke the best Portuguese. A pastor had
taken Mundico to Itacajá, where he was educated before
returning to the village. I wasn't sure if Buell Quain was
referring to him (the pastor or Mundico himself) when
he mentioned in his report on the Krahô 'the influence
of a particularly sophisticated 35-year-old man who taught
Brazilian dances to the Indians'. Diniz was only a boy, and
he watched the anthropologist with curiosity. He observed
everything. The village had recently been established in
that place, which they called Cabeceira Grossa. Quain
counted 210 inhabitants. The day after he arrived, he
went to the river to bathe, and Diniz, who was watching

him, saw him scratch his head. The ethnologist did not eat with the Indians and declined their food. He did not eat their tapioca. He had his own rice. On one occasion, he assisted a childbirth, named the newborn, and brought presents. But he didn't usually participate in village life. He wrote for days on end. 'He smoked like a chimney. Rope tobacco,' the old man said. Did he drink? 'No. He didn't drink.' He played records for the village and sang. One boy sang the village songs to him. 'His name was Zacarias. He's dead,' the old man said. I asked if he knew why Buell Quain had killed himself. 'I think he went mad after receiving some letters. He said his wife had betrayed him, with his brother. After that all he did was pack his things, that was all, he didn't talk to anybody. One day, not long after he received the letters, he said he was leaving. He hired two boys, João Canuto and Ismael – they're both dead – and went out to the courtyard and said goodbye. They left in the morning.'

The contradictions between the official version and Diniz's account had mainly to do with dates, causes, and effects. According to the old man, the three of them arrived in a marshy area towards the end of the afternoon, a place with some sort of running water, probably a stream, and the ethnologist asked them to stop. He said he couldn't go on, he was too tired. He thought the landscape pretty, 'a charming place to rest', as Manoel Perna wrote to Dona Heloísa. Perna based his story on what the apprehensive Indians told him when they arrived in Carolina a week later. The local representative of the

Banco do Brasil, Carlos Dias, confirmed this in a letter to Rio de Janeiro. The only difference from Diniz's version was that according to Diniz everything happened that first night. If they really left the village on the 31st, and assuming they were covering around thirty kilometres a day, they would already have been on the road for three days, since they were still ninety kilometres from Carolina. According to the official version, the anthropologist killed himself on the night of the 2nd. However, in one of her letters, his mother mentions her son's death came at the end of an inglorious attempt to reach civilization after four days' march. 'They stopped in the forest. He said he couldn't go on. They two boys made him a straw hut,' old Diniz said. It was there, at the end of the afternoon and with night already falling, that Buell Quain wrote his last letters, 'sobbing copiously', according to Manoel Perna's account. He gave João Canuto a note and instructed him to take it to the nearest ranch. The Indian obeyed. The other boy supposedly remained with the ethnologist, asleep. There are also internal contradictions in Diniz's story. But these are only to be expected in repeating a story heard in childhood, sixty years before, none of whose particulars he personally witnessed. According to him, for example, Quain 'started cutting himself all over, even during the day, and blood was pouring from him' and, later, he 'burned money' while writing his letters. This suggests that the anthropologist had gone mad. In the official version, he burned all the letters he received, leaving no clues to the reasons for his suicide. 'He mentioned nothing about the correspondence he received – the letters that so upset him – never revealing their contents to the Indians, and burned them after reading them, reducing them to ashes,' wrote Carlos Dias, the banker of Carolina, in an explanatory letter to Heloísa Alberto Torres. Quain slashed his neck and arms. But if he started to mutilate himself during the day, as old Diniz told me, how could the Indian Ismael not have noticed? After all, Ismael was with him while the other went to deliver his note to the nearest ranch. In the official reports, Ismael was asleep and fled when he awoke to the hellish sight of Quain covered with blood. João Canuto wasn't aware of the contents of the note he delivered to Balduíno, owner of the Serrinha ranch. Balduíno was out when the Indian arrived. Nobody there knew how to read. In the note, the anthropologist asked for a shovel and a hoe to dig a grave, since he wished to be buried there on the spot, 'in the same place where he died'. When he returned to the site with neither shovel nor hoe, João Canuto found him covered with knife wounds and blood. Horrified, he begged the anthropologist to stop hurting himself, imploring him not to do that, not to die. He was shocked by his deplorable state. He asked why Quain was doing that to himself, and the delirious man replied that 'he had to put an end to his suffering, to do away with his excruciating pain', since he could no longer carry on, since he couldn't face returning to Carolina. Neither account makes clear if the shame he referred to in his despair referred to his wife's hypothetical betrayal or if, wounded in his ill-timed suicide attempt, he couldn't face the people there. Upon seeing the Indian return, he seemed to regain consciousness for a moment. After his act of insanity, he realized there was no way back. Frightened, João fled as well. He went back to the Serrinha ranch in search of help. When he came back the following morning, accompanied by Balduíno, the landowner, and some of his employees, they found the ethnologist hanging from a bent tree, above a pool of blood. 'When the Indians fled, he hanged himself from a thick, bowed tree with cord from his hammock,' old Diniz said. He was buried at that spot, as he had requested. They dug him a grave and, after he was buried, marked the place with palm stalks. No local authority or policeman visited the scene. The body was not exhumed. No inquest was filed in any archive or in the public records of Carolina or Pedro Afonso. At the Carolina police station, records predating 1980 have been burned. Heloísa Alberto Torres's requests to mark the grave in case the family ever wished to pay their respects to the dead man went unheeded. As far as anyone knows, no one has ever returned there.

Quain didn't have a brother. Before I went to Carolina, at the beginning of August, I tried to locate Manoel Perna's family, and discovered his oldest daughter, Raimunda, in the telephone directory. She was listed as living in Miracema do Tocantins. She reported that the Indians told her father that the reason Quain committed suicide was that he had discovered that his wife was cheating on him with his brother. It was a shock to hear that for the first time, all the more so because I knew that among the letters he left behind was one addressed to his sister's husband – and none for his sister or his mother. When I mentioned this to the anthropologist whose newspaper article had first sparked my interest, she observed that for the Indians the terms *brother* and *brother-in-law* could have a symbolic or 'classificatory' meaning. In other words, they relate to the transmission of names rather than describe blood relationships. Brother or brother-in-law, according to her, could refer to just a friend, someone from Quain's social circle. And I had to remind her that as far as we knew, he didn't have a wife. Quain might have claimed to be married for entirely pragmatic reasons, to protect his privacy. (That is surely the only reason he would have said he was married in the form requesting permission for his research, sent to the Supervisory Committee for Artistic and Scientific Expeditions on his arrival in Brazil. And he might have told the Indians the same thing for the same reason: to avoid uncomfortable questions or situations.) But he might indeed have been referring to another person – and why not his own sister?

When I later told this story to a sceptical friend, he said, laughing: 'Impossible. It would be very Rodriguian,' referring to the incest theme running through the plays of Nelson Rodrigues. Quain's niece and nephew were born in 1928 and 1932, respectively. That means that his sister had been married since Quain was a teenager, and his brother-in-law would have been part of the family for more than a decade when Buell killed himself. It's hard to believe that some new turn in the brother-in-law's behaviour could have been enough to drive the anthropologist to suicide. The possibility that his brother-in-law could have cheated on Quain's sister with another woman, which can't be ruled out, remains an implausible reason for the suicide. Just after Buell's death, his mother went on holiday with her daughter's family in Oregon, and she makes no mention of an affair in her letters. True, she was not the kind of woman to wring the truth out of the people around her, nor let others do it for her. But it's still hard to believe that she would seek refuge from her sadness and loneliness by spending time with a presumed cause of her son's suicide. If something had happened, she would have let it be known, whether by gesture or by word.

It's still a mystery why one of Quain's seven last letters was addressed to his brother-in-law. He didn't write to his mother or sister. Only the men in the family. Perhaps these letters asked his father and brother-in-law to take care of his mother and sister, since he would no longer be there for them. But the idea that he had an ambiguous relationship with his sister, though entirely hypothetical, was a suspicion I couldn't quite shake.

On 13 September 1939, Marion Quain Kaiser, Buell's sister, wrote, from Chicago, an extremely odd letter to Ruth Benedict:

Since my mother has already written to you, I haven't felt that I needed to. But your letter that arrived today, addressed to my mother, convinced me that I need to clear up the matter of Buell's will, if I can. First of all, my father, who wrote to you from Seattle, managed more or less to estrange himself from the family when he divorced my mother for no good reason last winter. He was never interested in Buell's work or plans. I'm afraid this tragedy has not affected him as it has us. Yet the fact that Buell wanted his investments to come to you worried my father, since he was always very interested in MONEY.

Once again, after Quain's death, the issue was money. In the letter he left Ruth Benedict on his death – the one he asked her to disinfect before reading, just as he had in the letter he wrote to Dona Heloísa at the same time ('I have a fever that may be contagious. Sterilize this letter') – the ethnologist wrote:

I'm going to die. I apologize for failing so dreadfully in the Brazilian project after worrying you so much about it. But I'm sure that it's for the best. Much work can still be done in Brazil – I wish you the best of luck, and send you personally all my affection. I need to ask you (I'm sorry about this) if, besides the 4,000 dollars I spent in Brazil and which belong to you, you would let my sister and my niece have the rest of my money, since they are broke and need it. You will receive this letter long after my death. The Indians are safe, which is a source of satisfaction to me.

Safe from what? Or from whom?

Much of the money he left came from an insurance policy. In her letter to Benedict, Marion expressed her irritation at the suggestion that something in one of her letters could have pushed him to suicide:

> I can't understand why Buell suddenly decided I needed his money. I only hope that the story about the letters that so upset him turns out to be false. But the note he sent you leads me to believe that he thought he'd be most useful to everyone if he were dead. Under normal circumstances, I know Buell would not have been so foolish. The thought that some nonsense I may have written might have set off this whole thing makes me sick. The fact is, none of us will probably ever know, which makes it all the harder for us to move past it. I'm not broke and I'm certainly not in desperate need of money. Buell himself knew that very well.

Marion asked Ruth Benedict to keep the money and to use it for anthropological research, as her brother had wished. 'At least Buell's work will be published, and other research might also be supported by his money.' She added to the letter a handwritten document in which she ceded all her rights to any of her brother's investments to Ruth Benedict. 'My father is very capable of faking elevated sentiments when he stands to gain from them. Please, don't let him or anyone else interfere with the lawful will.'

We left Carolina in the morning, in a four-wheel-drive pick-up truck. The anthropologist drove, seated beside a half-black Krahô and his white wife, the three of them seated in a covered cabin, protected from the sun and the dust. Behind, unsheltered, I travelled with the anthropologist's son and a group of ten Indians, alongside backpacks, suitcases, provisions, plastic bags full of raw meat exposed to the sun, and other assorted junk. I stood silently, my eyes fixed on the horizon. Somewhere, a few kilometres to our right, according to the none too detailed or accurate map I had brought, was the grave of Buell Quain, forgotten in the middle of the woods. The sun, the wind, and the rains had swept away the dried stalks of palm long ago.

We travelled through the scrubby forest for five hours, crossing rivers and sandbanks. Eventually, the earthen path began to run parallel to the Red River, which we crossed on foot, in waist-high water and with our luggage on our heads. But there we were, only half a kilometre from the New Village. The whole town was waiting for us on the riverbank. They had heard the noise of the truck. Indians hear everything. The Red River is green. The Indians had long drunk from those waters, using them for fishing and bathing, until the day when their teeth began to fall out, one after the other, and they started dying for no apparent reason. Some managed to reach the city, where they died in hospital, before the perplexed and uncomprehending doctors. At that point they decided to stop using water from the Red River and began to bathe in and drink from a stream that ran on the other side of the village, and started to fish in a distant lake. Eventually they discovered what had poisoned the Red River. A hospital upstream, in Recursolândia, was dumping its waste into the water. That is what they told me as soon as I arrived and looked at me silently, with imploring eyes, as if there were anything I could do about it.

Before we left Carolina, I asked the anthropologist where I would stay. He said the Indians would decide once we reached the village. Before we even crossed the river, one of the Krahô who was riding in the back of the pick-up came forward and said I would stay in his house. His name was José Maria Teinõ and he looked something like an early-twentieth-century Mexican guerrilla, with a moustache, very dark skin, and wavy shoulder-length hair. A puny boy with shining eyes was waiting for him. It was his son. I never learned the boy's name or age (he must have been around ten), though, in a way, it was he who came closest to telling me something like the truth. Before I realized what he was doing, he had seized my backpack and begun to forge across the river, the pack on his head in the chest-high water. When he reached the far side, he headed up a high bluff beside the river to the bicycle he had left there. He was acting on the orders of his father, my host, despite my objections to the grotesque sight of this small, scrawny boy carrying my backpack while I, a grown man, travelled empty-handed. For them it was a matter of courtesy. We were surrounded by dozens of Indians, modest but

curious, who said things I couldn't understand and
laughed. From the top of the opposite bank, it was only
about five hundred metres to the village. This comprised
twenty houses, built of adobe and roofed with straw,
arranged around a central yard. The town is arranged in
a sun-like or wagon-wheel pattern, with tamped-down
dirt paths connecting, like rays, the houses to the central
courtyard. There were few trees, and the Indians had
planted them themselves. They had only been there for
around eight years. The previous village was dismantled
when one group decided to move to the New Village and
the rest, unhappy with the chosen site, joined the Red
River village, the one we had seen from a distance on
the road. The previous site had been abandoned because
it had become infertile. I don't know how much super-
stition was involved in the decision. They said the ground
was bad. They mentioned the number of Indians who
were buried there. When she saw me, José Maria's wife,
Antônia Jàtcaprec, grimaced. Later they told me it was
nothing personal. She came across as both fearless and
cantankerous. She was very thin, with drawn cheeks and
thin lips. My visit meant that they would have to
rearrange the house to free up one of the rooms for me.
As I entered, I smelled the pestilential stench of dried
fish strung up in the middle of the room. The odour
penetrated everything. By the second day, I not only was
not used to it, I couldn't stand so much as a whiff of it.

Nine people slept in the house. As it was the dry
season, their summer, the couple slept on a raised bunk,

beneath a canopy. The children slept in hammocks in the
front room, where the wretched-smelling fish were also
hung. There were two other rooms. In one, the two oldest
daughters slept with their infants. I didn't immediately
understand where their husbands were, if they had them.
I hung my hammock in the other room. The floor
consisted of packed earth. The nights were a festival of
intimate noises, snores, farts, and crying children. In the
front room, the boys in their hammocks thrashed in their
nightmares. On my last night, another daughter and her
husband, who had been travelling when I arrived, joined
the two sisters and their nursing babies, piled up in the
room next to mine. And the sighs of sex joined the cries
of the children.

Towards the end of the afternoon we arrived, just after
I had moved in, I set out in search of the anthropologist
and his son, who were staying in another house. I found
them wearing shorts and flip-flops (when in Rome . . .),
their bodies painted with annatto dye, seated in front of
the house of the shaman, Afonso Cupõ. Afonso was an
enormous man, always smiling, with a kind-hearted face,
who generally didn't say much. The next day, however,
when he was drunk, he cornered me and made me promise
to give him fifty *reais* before I left. Fortunately for me,
he had completely forgotten about it the next day. His
wife, Cajari, was stretched out on a mat on the ground,
as if chatting with her friends on the beach. And their
sons Leusipo Pempxà and Neno Mãhi, two strong men
in their twenties, were listening to the conversation in

silence, waving off the skeletal, mangy dogs that occasionally approached. Waving off dogs is one of the most notable activities of daily life in the village, and it is pursued from infancy into age. The Krahô prove that dogs are not man's best friend but rather one of the most imbecilic creatures that has ever walked the face of the earth. No matter how badly they are treated by their owners, who use them for hunting, the dogs never leave. When they are beaten or stoned – which happens whenever they get within a foot of a person – they run off howling, but then immediately return to beg for leftover food. Neno had been hit by a truck in somewhat obscure circumstances and wore a plastic brace that served as an orthopaedic vest. The shaman's oldest daughter had been taken to a hospice in a nearby town. She had gone mad. I thought it funny to see the anthropologist and his son covered head-to-toe in body paint. I laughed at them, but not for long. I stopped as soon as I saw their puzzled expressions. They were surprised at my naiveté. They felt sorry for me. They didn't say anything. They didn't want to frighten me. That was just the beginning. The next day it would be my turn.

At seven that night, the boy with the bicycle came to summon me to dinner. Every guest ate in the house they were staying in, which meant, to my dismay, that I would be eating separately from the anthropologist and his son. My first dinner in the village (a plate of rice covered with pieces of, and a soup made from, the fish I had seen hanging inside the house) was a warning. As we sat – José Maria, his wife, his two daughters with their small children, the boy with the bicycle, and I – at the back of the house, in a kind of yard around a small brazier in which they warmed up that dry subspecies of bottom-feeding lungfish, Antônia spoke to me for the first time. She handed me an agate plate topped with rice and fish and asked me if I thought the village was ugly. She was unhappy living there. She had preferred the old village and wanted to see São Paulo. I hardly heard her. I was trying to chew the pestilential fish, a mass of bones and fins that I finally ended up swallowing whole. I exclaimed how delicious it was and prayed to God that I wouldn't throw up in front of my hosts. On the very first day, that wouldn't have looked good. I tried to dissuade her from the idea of São Paulo, asking what she would want to do in such a violent and ugly place. And I ate as much as I could, which wasn't much, soon awakening the concern of my hosts. Thus began an alimentary *via crucis*. I only managed to swallow the fish on one other occasion, at breakfast the following day, since the same vittles were served at every meal. Concerned that I was only eating rice, José Maria went in search of the anthropologist, and returned with the suggestion that they serve me food besides the dried fish, vegetables, for instance, which I loved. At the next meal, they handed me a plate of sweet potatoes. For a moment, I confess, I was happy and relieved. I started to peel the first potato (there were five on my plate) and took an initial mouthful, under the anxious eyes of my hosts. My mouth filled with dirt. Only then did I realize that the potatoes consisted of various pieces and had been cooked just as they had been dug up, with the dirt mixed into the soft mass of tubers, like a chocolate layer cake. I chewed the potatoes and the dirt and said: 'Mmm! How delicious!', but as soon as they turned their backs I started throwing almost everything on my plate into the forest, to the delight of the dogs, who in their eagerness for my leftovers ended up blowing my cover. 'It wasn't good?' asked Antônia. 'It was great. But I'm just not very hungry. I need to lose some weight,' I said, handing the plate back to her with the two remaining potatoes, still unpeeled. José Maria instantly devoured them.

I had brought along some granola bars just in case, concealed in the bottom of my backpack. As soon as I arrived and José Maria and his son with the bicycle gathered around me to see what was in the backpack, I managed to remain one step ahead of them, saying that everything inside would be a gift for them when I left. I wanted to avoid any awkwardness. But I hid the granola bars. I only had ten. In the middle of my first night, I crawled out of my hammock one foot at a time, opened my backpack, and took out a bar. There were a thousand noises all around at night, but as soon as I tore open the wrapper the most absolute silence seemed to descend upon the village and only I, and with the annoying rustling of that packaging, could be heard. I took a bite and the sound of my chewing rang out like a thunderclap. I stuffed the whole thing into my mouth and waited for it to soften, chewing slowly and deliberately. The next day, when I met my hosts for breakfast, they asked if I had slept well, if the hammock was comfortable. While she was serving me that blessed fish, Antônia said that she had been worried, thinking I was cold when I got up in the middle of the night, but that she had put it out of her head when she saw I had only got up to eat. Now I had no choice. I went inside, took out the nine remaining granola bars, and brought them out to breakfast. They devoured them all in less than five minutes, repeating the word 'chocolate' as they ate.

Between ten in the morning and two in the afternoon it was impossible to remain outside. There was almost no shade. I decided to sit in the central room, beneath the overhanging fish, and read a book. But my peace did not last long. First, the youngest son of the shaman showed up, Neno Māhi, the one with the plastic brace that I had seen the night before. This time he wasn't wearing the brace. He came to tell me about the accident. He said he needed a lawyer so he could sue the truck driver. He said he was hit and abandoned on the road, as if it had all happened the night before. The driver fled the scene, but he knew who he was. I had barely arrived in the village. I was shocked by his story and sympathized with him. Neno said he would never work again. He wanted to sue for damages. Later, when I repeated the story to the anthropologist, he told me that that wasn't exactly how it happened. I realized that as the most recent arrival I was becoming the village idiot, an easy target for stories nobody else still believed. I sat for hours listening to his chatter, unsure exactly what the Indian wanted from me. As he wouldn't leave, I eventually decided to return to my reading. After a few minutes, faced with my stillness and silence, he got up and left. But the silence lasted no more than a few minutes, because at that point his brother Leusipo Pempxà came in. He came into the half-light of the doorway, an indistinct shape. His face reminded me of those evil South American Indians in the *Adventures of Tintin*. His hooked nose, his high forehead above his deep eyes, the sunken cheeks bordered by his smooth, black, shoulder-length hair. It was hard for me to understand what these people wanted. Leusipo asked what I was doing in the village. I decided to take this as a friendly question and, in my naive paternalism, began to explain to him what a novel was. He wasn't interested. He wanted to know what I was doing in the village. The elders were worried, they wanted to know what I was doing digging around in the past. He didn't like it when the elders got worried. I tried to convince him that there was no cause for them to worry. Everything I wanted to find out about was already known. And he asked: 'So why do you want to know, if you already know?' I tried to explain to him that I wanted to write a book and explained once more what a novel was, a book of fiction (I showed him what I had in my hands), that it would all be just a story, without any repercussions in the real world. He still wouldn't believe me. He acted offended, but all he really wanted to do was intimidate me. I was partly annoyed, partly frightened. I wanted to tell the Indian to fuck off, but I couldn't alienate the village. If there was anything to learn there (and Leusipo's attempt to intimidate me suggested there was), I had to go about it diplomatically. He wanted to know what I was doing there. As at the Timbira assembly in Carolina, I didn't have enough information to decide if he really knew something or if he didn't know anything at all and was just as curious as I was. Leusipo was not about to lay off. He didn't smile, and he made no friendly gesture or expression. He had an implacable, determined look in his eye. He had come to intimidate me. He repeated: 'The elders are worried.' And I thought to myself: 'This idiot must have heard something and decided to take his chance to get back at me.' My explanations about my novel were useless. I tried to explain that, for white people who didn't believe in the gods, fiction was like myth, the equivalent of the Indians' myths, and before I finished the sentence I no longer knew which one of us was the idiot. He didn't say anything except: 'Why are you digging around in the past?' He repeated the question. Faced with his bovine stubbornness, I finally realized that I didn't know the answer to his question. I couldn't make him understand what fiction was (in fact he wasn't interested), or convince him that my interest could have no real consequences, that in the end it would all be made up anyway. I was rescued by José Maria's oldest daughter, who must have been around eighteen and showed up holding a greasy ball of annatto, to paint me. On any other occasion, I would have fought like a pig on its way to the slaughterhouse. But my willingness to struggle was limited by the circumstances. I wasn't at all happy about it, but I agreed to take off my shirt. I would have done anything to get rid of Leusipo. And indeed, as soon as the girl entered, with her back turned to him as if he were no more than an animal, my inquisitor immediately got up from the bench he had sat on, uninvited, at my side, and left. He was irritated by the interruption and left the house like a reproached dog when José Maria arrived to admire the paint his daughter had spread across my body with her oily, red-dyed hands. They thought it was great entertainment to see me all red. Everything I touched also turned red: the book I was reading, my shorts, my backpack, my hat. The tinge of annatto dye. But that was nothing compared to the genipap dye that awaited me the next day.

From then on, I tried to dodge Leusipo and his brother. I avoided being alone with either of them. And when I left to bathe early in the morning, I prayed they wouldn't be there. But they never bothered me again. Most of the Indians didn't speak to me. They either ignored me or observed me at a distance. They might have been wary, or they might simply not have been interested. When they approached, it was either to ask me for something or because they were drunk. Only the children laughed at me, and the women. The women and children were the liveliest. They said things to each other that I couldn't understand and laughed. They called me white man: 'Cupen, cupen.' They made fun of me. Slowly, I found out that, with the exception of my hostess, the women in the village were more spirited, good-humoured, and intelligent than the men, who shut them out of important decisions. They were constantly laughing and joking, while the men observed them silently, not understanding or not seeing the humour, unable to tell a joke themselves, envying the women's vivacity. I could never tell when the men were drunk. Almost all of the villagers were blood relatives. I gradually discovered that the New Village was practically one single family, that they were almost all brothers and sisters, uncles and aunts and nieces and nephews, and that their symbolic, classificatory associations mainly served to mask relationships that if not incestuous were at least somewhat questionable. I never managed to comprehend either the blood relations or the symbolic relations between the members of the tribe. They were very complex, and my aims were not anthropological. Quain himself had trouble understanding how it all worked. I understood nothing. I didn't know what would happen next. I saw that they were busy preparing something, but I had no idea what, or what role I was meant to have in the ceremonies, which only heightened my sense of expectation and fear. The anthropologist had bought a pig to celebrate his son's recovery. The Indians prepared a *paparuto*, a kind of manioc cake stuffed with lard and pieces of pork. In the afternoon, I watched the women work. They were laying banana leaves across the ground on a mat of tree branches and covering them with the manioc paste they had been preparing since the day before. On top of that, they spread the pork and lard. As I was watching them, I felt a presence, a shadow behind me, a slight vibration in the air, a breath on my neck. When I turned around, the phantasmagoric figure of the elderly Vicente Hintxuatyc, the village patriarch and the symbolic brother of João Canuto, was standing with his face practically touching mine. He was almost sniffing me, and bore the same indecipherable and threatening look with which Leusipo had tried to intimidate me that morning. I started, but thanks to a wit and an inner control I don't usually possess, didn't display anything except an inquisitive expression. I looked at the wrinkled old man with his shaggy greying hair, and casually asked him what he wanted. He continued to stare at me in silence before moving off without a word. Vicente had been a boy during the time Buell Quain lived among the Krahô, but he never met him. He wasn't living in the village at the time. He had spent much time among the whites, coming and going, and only returned to the Krahô in old age. He had been in the village during the massacre of 1940 and barely escaped. In some way or another, they were all trying to intimidate me, even if only for their amusement, and that only frightened me the more and made me suspect they really were hiding something.

They began cooking the *paparuto* that same night, while the women secretly prepared the anthropologist's son. At

the end of the afternoon, they cut his hair in the Krahô
fashion, with two parallel stripes at the sides and a short
fringe at the front. They painted his body with genipap,
spreading a resin across his torso, legs, and arms, and
then covered him with grey and white feathers.
Meanwhile, the men dug a hole in the earth for use as
an oven. Around eight in the evening, after they had strewn
the lard and the pork over the manioc paste, the women
covered the *paparuto* with the banana leaves and the men
carried it to the cooking hole. They covered it with stones
and earth under the gaze of the entire tribe, including the
anthropologist's son, already adorned, his father, who was
taking pictures, and me. For the first time I had a clearer
sense, seeing the boy covered with feathers and painted
black, that my time could come too. That afternoon, the
women had already tried to paint me with genipap. I put
them off, saying that the annatto was enough. They simply
laughed among themselves and said things I couldn't
understand. Despite my growing apprehension, the night
was one of the most beautiful I had ever seen. The full
moon illuminated the village in silvery light. Nobody
needed lanterns or candles. There was a bonfire in the
central courtyard, around which the men sat talking until
late. An old Krahô singer, who had been summoned from
another village especially for the festivities, sang, accompanied by the women, beneath the indolent gaze of their
husbands, fathers, and brothers seated on the ground.
Slowly, as the ceremony advanced into the night, the
Indians began to leave for their houses, until nobody but

the singer was left in the centre of the village. I went to
sleep around eleven, knowing that the *paparuto* would be
dug up before sunrise. I slept, soothed by the voice of the
old Krahô singer, who continued to return to the centre
of the village to sing his songs. There was something
marvellous and enchanting in the ritual. Around three in
the morning, hearing the old singer once more, I decided
to get up and go and see. And I came upon one of the
most stunning sights of my life. The old man sang alone
in the middle of the immobile, sleeping village. After a
few minutes, a woman appeared in the doorway of a house
and silently emerged, a vague figure in the distance. She
walked down one of the paths that led to the centre of
the village. The solitary figure advanced slowly, wrapped
in rags to protect herself from the cold. When she reached
the village centre, she came up to the cantor and joined
him in his song, as if they were a duet. Minutes later,
another woman emerged from the door of another house
and walked the solitary path that led to the centre. From
each of the houses, one woman after another, at intervals
of some minutes, came towards the old singer and stood
in a line in front of him, to accompany him. He called
them one at a time, until there was a full choir of women
under his leadership and the full moon. As they arrived
and took their places in the choir, the voices gathered and
penetrated the other houses. After a while, a man emerged
with a small baby. And taking the same path his wife had
walked before, he came to the centre of the village, stopped
in front of his mother, whose breasts were now outside

the rags, and gave her the child. Then he went back to
his house. The Krahô treat children with special defer-
ence. And even when they reproach them, they do so
lightheartedly.

At five in the morning, they began to unearth the
paparuto. I had returned to my hammock, where I was
awakened by movement in the house. Adults and children were emerging from all the houses and heading for
the village centre, where the *paparuto* was to be divvied
up. Each family received their share and returned to eat
it at home. Still at the centre of the village, the old singer
kindly offered me a portion. The lard had melted during
the night and soaked into the manioc layer, which was
now a fatty blob, upon which lay the pieces of pork. I
took a bite of the glistening cake – in which the occasional pig hair could still be seen, and from which the
lard oozed over my fingers – and said: 'Hummm!' before
returning it to the old man. He laughed and asked if I
didn't like it, pressing me to eat more. I ate the whole
thing, which sank into my empty stomach like a rock. I
fell sick. I had hardly eaten since I arrived in the village,
and now that chunk of lard for breakfast. Everyone took
a share and returned home. The sun was already up and
it was starting to get hot. Only a few mangy dogs remained
in the village centre, hoping for any possible leftovers,
licking at the lard mixed with dirt lying on the banana
leaves. My hosts had gathered behind the house to savour
the *paparuto*. They called me over, but I said that I
couldn't eat any more and stretched out in my hammock.

I felt nauseous and as soon as I stood up everything started to spin. My state was made worse by the nervous feeling that after they finished with the anthropologist's son it would be my turn. I had no strength to resist when the women arrived in the afternoon to paint me with genipap. Genipap dye is a transparent liquid containing small pieces of the fruit, and when applied to the skin it colours it black. The riper the fruit, the darker the hue. Unlike annatto, genipap does not stain clothes. What they didn't tell me at the time, and which I should have been able to work out, is that it doesn't stain clothing because it never leaves the skin. No amount of scrubbing will remove it. Genipap remains on the skin for an entire month. Since the dye is transparent, I had no idea what they were painting on my body. When they were done, they gave me a bamboo cane in case I needed to scratch or dispel the mosquitoes before the paint was dry. I was warned not to touch my body with my hands for the first twelve hours, while the dye was still active, in order not to stain my hands. When I awoke the following morning, I was covered with black designs, large, geometric, zigzag lines. By going along with the genipap I had made a first, unintentional gesture of respect and friendship. Before eight in the morning they came to get me. Only when I arrived in the central square did I understand that they were meeting to decide my fate. The women were not present. The men were discussing matters in their language. I tried to stay close to the anthropologist and his son, in hopes of some translation,

but suddenly, without my understanding why, they separated into two groups, like football teams, and anthropologist and his son were split up, one on each side of
the square. My fate was being decided without my partici-
pation. I stood alone in the middle. On one side stood
the summer or dry-season clan (Wakmêye), to which the
anthropologist belonged. On the other was the winter or
rainy-season clan (Katamye), to which José Maria and
the anthropologist's son belonged. The two groups alter-
nated the administration of the village, like two political
parties. The old singer approached and told me that I
now had to choose which clan I wanted to join. On either
side the Indians were shouting things I couldn't understand but which I took to mean that if I didn't choose
their team they would cut off my head, skin me alive,
tear out all my hair, etc. They screamed and laughed.
José Maria insisted that I was staying in his house and
that I had to choose his side. I didn't know what to do.
The anthropologist shouted that he had brought me to
the village and that I had to stay with him, and that is
what I – spinelessly – ended up doing. I have always
preferred summer, I don't like rain, I tried to explain to
José Maria as we returned back to his house. But nothing
could lesson his disappointment. 'From now on, I'm not
speaking to you. You betrayed me. You made your choice,
now deal with it,' he answered. I tried to convince myself
that it was all a big game to them, but that didn't help.
In the middle of the afternoon, the two groups headed
into the forest in search of logs for the race. All I wanted

was not to have to participate in anything. The log race
is one of the ancient traditions of the Krahô. It is a relay
race in which a palm log, which must weigh fifty kilos,
is carried on the shoulders. The first group to reach the
village centre win. I grew even more apprehensive after
the race, of which I only saw the final sprint, when I
decided to bathe in the stream and was prevented by my
hosts. 'No! You can't! Today, you're going to bathe in the
village centre.' I ran off in search of the anthropologist
and asked him what awaited me. But he wouldn't answer
me directly, saying that I would have to wait and see,
that it was a 'fun' event. I returned to the house, terrified. Things only got worse when the boy with the bicycle,
José Maria's son, came up to me and managed only to
say: 'They're lying to you.' He had to interrupt what he
was about to tell me, pedalling off and disappearing when
he saw his father approaching, the latter eyeing his son's
familiarity with me suspiciously. I couldn't get the phrase
out of my head. It was the closest I had come to any
kind of truth. I didn't know if he meant they were lying
about what they were planning for me that evening, or
if they were hiding something from me about the past
and the death of Quain. It was terrible in either case. By
then I had a splitting headache. My head was throbbing
as if it were about to explode. There was no way I could
be alone with the bicycle boy again, to ask him what he
meant. I was feverish, lying in my hammock, when at
nightfall José Maria summoned me to the centre of the
village. I went unwillingly, light-headed and horrified,

without knowing what awaited me there, or what sort of 'bath' they had in mind. I put on a pair of boxers under my shorts, just in case. It was already pretty cold, and I didn't want to get my clothes wet. I saw the men gathered around the bonfire. I had the impression that everyone except me knew what was about to happen. Old Vicente invited me to sit next to him and spontaneously began to talk about Quain, whom he hadn't actually known. He didn't tell me anything I didn't already know. But he at least seemed more trusting. I wasn't really interested in the things he was telling me. I was hardly listening. I was shaky and weak, whether from hunger or fear I don't know. Finally, the anthropologist arrived, and I, who can't have been looking too good, begged him to tell me once and for all what was about to happen. 'You made up your mind this morning. Now you're going to meet your family, all the women you can't have sex with,' he said. I didn't want to meet anybody. I was about to pass out when the women showed up, with buckets and bottles filled with water. A circle of men, holding hands, sang and danced around the bonfire, under the guidance of the old singer. I was trying to protect myself by sticking with the anthropologist. Suddenly, the old singer pushed me towards the circle of men. I resisted, saying I had a fever, and I couldn't bathe in the cold. He laughed, saying that the bath would cure the fever. There was nothing I could do. I simply asked if I could take off my shirt, my shorts, and my sandals. As soon as I came into the circle in my boxer shorts, the women approached, carrying their bottles and buckets, surrounding the circle of men. We danced around the fire, holding hands. The Indians sang. I expected the worst. Suddenly, the dancing and the singing stopped. A few women approached with buckets and bottles, picked out a few men and took them to the middle of the ring, near the fire. The men bowed their heads, as if in prayer, while the women, laughing heartily, dumped water on their heads. That was when I understood what the ritual was about, though I still didn't understand why it was being performed or what it had to do with me. The women poured water on the men they were symbolically related to, the men with whom they could not have sexual relations. The bath was a ceremonial explication and delineation of the incest taboo. The first group of bathed men returned to the circle, and the women rejoined the others outside the circle. We all began to dance and sing. When the music stopped again, one of the women pushed me close to the fire, while others took hold of other men, and emptied a bucket of water on my head. My fever disappeared, as did my headache. If that was all there was too it, then great. Being close to the fire kept me warm and helped me dry off. I took two more baths and the circle broke up. I was relieved, thinking that was the end of it. I was ready to go home when the singer pushed me back to the fireside. A further ritual was about to begin. My fear returned, along with the idea that at some point, when I was most distracted, when I least expected it, they would all leap on top of me. The Indians arranged themselves in a new

pattern around the fire. The men formed lines that began
in the centre, by the fire, and extended out away from
it. They were no longer facing the fire but standing with
their sides towards it. They moved in a circular direction, one line following another, now clockwise, now
counter-clockwise. Seen with the bonfire, they formed a
solar arrangement, with the bonfire as the sun and the
men as the rays. They sang, led by the old singer, beside
themselves with laughter. I, in the middle of the whole
thing, asked the Indians beside me what the ritual meant.
'You don't know?' they answered, and laughed themselves
silly. Only later did they explain that each of the songs
told the story of a different animal, and that they all had
strong sexual connotations. With every new song, the
movement around the bonfire changed direction. Nothing
happened to me that night. But realizing that they would
soon want to baptize me (after all, why would they have
introduced me to the women of my 'family', if not to
prepare me for the giving of a new name?), I sought out
the anthropologist and told him as clearly as I knew how
that I was not about to be covered with feathers or have
my hair cut like a Krahô and that I would struggle to the
bitter end to defend myself. He must have been surprised
by my reaction and by my lack of sportsmanship. Only
after I saw what happened to him the following day did
I realize that he might have been sacrificed in my place.

The third night was hellish. It was bitterly cold and I
couldn't find a comfortable position in the hammock. Any
movement shifted the covers. At dawn, I heard a group of

men singing. They approached the house. I froze. They
came up, moved off, and then returned. I was sure they
were after me. Then they came to get me. I played dead.
I let everyone else get up and stayed in my hammock,
pretending to sleep. When I finally decided to get up, the
ritual was already well under way. They had got their hands
on the anthropologist. He was covered with feathers and
the Indians were carrying him on their shoulders over to
the stream for a morning baptism. It was strange that they
were baptizing him, since he had already been through
this years before. It took me a while to realize that he,
fearing my reaction, had probably taken the place reserved
for me, to spare them disappointment. When they brought
him back from the stream, he was surrounded by men and
women in the centre of the village. At that point the women
began to mock my cowardice. The woman who taunted
me the most forcefully, Gersila Kryjkwỳi, clearly did not
approve. I responded that I did not feel like being baptized.
I had only been in the village for three days. But I promised her that next time I would let them do whatever they
wanted with me. Gersila cried that she knew very well
that there would be no next time, and that I was a coward.
Creuza Prumkwỳi said that she would wait, then, and that
the next time I set foot in the village they would baptize
me strictly by the book, tearing out every one of my
eyelashes and my eyebrow hairs, that they would draw
blood. They all cracked up. I hate to boast, but I don't
think they'd ever had as much fun mocking a white man.
Before we left, old Vicente's wife, the village matriarch

Francelina Wrãmkwỳi came over. Francelina was the mother of them all, a hunchback, both fragile and strong, who had only death to look forward to and who reminded me of my 107-year-old grandmother. She said that she had been wary of me at first but that she had ended up liking me, and she knew I wouldn't forget the Indians. Despite all my terrifying experiences, I eventually felt a certain sympathy for them. And that was after only three days. I wondered how Quain would have felt after almost five months alone with the Krahô. On the way back, in the pick-up truck, the anthropologist tried to wean me from my doubts when I told him what the bicycle boy had whispered to me on the second afternoon, before being surprised by his father. The anthropologist assured me that they would have told him if there were any secrets about the American ethnologist. But he couldn't imagine how much of my mind was taken up by those secrets. Indeed, not even I could imagine it.

In letters he wrote to Margaret Mead at the beginning of July, which were discovered among the belongings the Indians brought to Carolina after his death, Quain complained about the difficulties of working with the Krahô:

> It's very difficult to train the natives here. The only way I can get them to do what I want is to get angry. Then, for the next twenty-four hours, I have all 210 of them at my feet, trying awkwardly to satisfy me. They have no notion of making an effort to earn or receive something,

since they usually get much more when they sulk. For the past month, I've been working with a young man (who is definitely abnormal, since he seems to like working with me) on the language. Today he told me that he could no longer work, since he was tired of being mocked by the rest of the village. Not even the children respect him.

Old Diniz didn't know who that informer might have been. He remembered the boy Zacarias, who sang for Quain, but not the young man the whole village scorned for working with the ethnologist.

The Indians adopt you when you come to their village. And they expect you to do the same when they come to the city. It is an apparently reciprocal relationship, but it is deeply strange and often disagreeable. It's not a relationship of equals, but of mutual adoption, which makes all the difference. In the village, you are their child; in the city, they are your children. I have never seen people who treat children with more tenderness or who give them more freedom. As soon as I got back to São Paulo, I started getting collect calls. Whenever they were in Carolina, the Indians called me. They asked for things. Mostly money. They didn't dress up their requests in any sort of ceremony. As if they were now my children. Their demands were endless. And I was eternally in their debt. I had been a child, and now I was suddenly like a lapsed father who finally has a chance to make up for his absences and past failures. It's hard to make sense of such a relationship.

They are the orphans of civilization. They are abandoned. They need allies in the white world, a world they make an effort, usually vain, to understand. And a relationship based on mutual adoption is by definition unbalanced, since the Krahô go to the whites much more often than the whites go to the Krahô. The world belongs to the whites. Their neediness is irremediable. They don't want to be forgotten. They attach themselves to anyone who comes through the village, as if visitors were long-lost parents. They want you to be part of the family. They need you to be a father, mother, and brother. In one of her letters to Dona Heloísa after her son's death, Fannie Quain said that the Krahô called him 'big brother' – this is not confirmed by other documents – and that they asked the authorities to send them a replacement for him as quickly as possible, someone with a soul as great as his. This paternal relationship is uncomfortable and irritating, as Quain himself found. There are those who don't have a problem with it. Not me. I am not an anthropologist and I don't have a great soul. I got fed up. After a while, I decided not to respond to the messages they left me, asking me to call urgently the following night. I was also irritated by my own guilt over this decision, but less so than I feared that at any minute they might knock on my door. Before I left the village, after I had refused to be baptized, Gersila approached me, acting half offended, half ironic, and told me I was no better than all the other whites, who had abandoned them, who never returned to the village, who never gave them a second thought. I swore that I would.

I was terrified of what they could do to me (even if it was only to cover me with feathers and give me a name and a family I could never again get rid of). My fear was apparent. I came over as rude. And they had laughed at my cowardice. I swore I would never forget them. And then I abandoned them, like all the other whites.

According to the story old Diniz told me, which was corroborated by the letter Buell Quain sent to Ruth Benedict on 15 September 1938, the young ethnologist was also wary of participating in or becoming involved in this type of relationship ('I don't like the idea of going native. The concessions I made, in Fiji, are here not only accepted but expected') and he didn't want another family. He already had one. It seems that he had more than enough reason to avoid these new ties. To judge by some of his last letters, they provoked his death.

For a while, after my interview with old Diniz, I was suspicious of the Indians' insistence that he hadn't had any kind of disease. How could they know? The two who reported his death to Manoel Perna as well as to old Diniz, who was then only a child, emphatically rejected any notion that he had come down with a contagious disease, as if that would suggest that they were somehow involved in his death. In his notes on the Krahô, Quain refers to 'introduced diseases':

The state of public health in the village requires urgent attention from the government. Besides the common cold, the serious diseases are tuberculosis, leprosy, and probably syphilis. My uncertainty about syphilis is due to the lack of advanced symptoms of the disease, such as Parkinson's disease, ataxia, or paresis. Most of the symptoms I have observed could be caused by tuberculosis.

Obsessed, he may have been seeing himself everywhere.

12

*You want to know what Dr Buell was doing in the village.
Probably nothing. And even if there were something, you
wouldn't get an answer out of the Indians. I don't know
anything either. But I can imagine, and so can you, as I
imagined it every time he told one of his stories. His loneliness was so intense that I imagined that on the night of his
suicide he was in flight.*

*When he returned to Carolina, more than two months
after having left with the Indians and more than two months
before his suicide, he was in a deplorable state. He wanted
to hide. He said he didn't trust anyone. But he can't have
mistrusted me, because he sought me out. He must have
remembered that first night he came to my house, as soon as
he got to the city, when he spoke to me of the Trumai. He
arrived dirty and shoeless. He was ashamed, intimidated by
the whites he had earlier derided. Afraid he couldn't express
himself, he no longer dared address them in Portuguese. I
was the only one who heard him. So he came to my house.
He preferred not to speak to the others. When he came looking
for me, it was to talk. Sometimes, when he was drinking, he
didn't make any sense. He thought they were after him, that
wherever he went they would find him. He didn't see a way
out. I asked, but he didn't say who 'they' were. He told me
he had lived under surveillance in Rio de Janeiro. He meant*

that he was being watched wherever he went. They knew everything he did, no matter how he tried to hide, no matter how secretive he was, no matter how discreet. And then he stopped speaking, took another drink and suddenly went back to what he was saying. He thought there was an information network in Brazil. The police in Rio or the inspectors of the Indian Protection Service were not the only things that frightened him. He said that since he arrived in Brazil his every step had been monitored. I had never seen anyone so alone. During his stay in Carolina, he came to my house in the late afternoon and we talked into the night. I often didn't understand what he was saying, but I nevertheless understood what he was trying to say. I imagined it. He just needed to talk with someone. On one occasion when he was telling me about his travels around the world, I asked him what he was trying to find and he said he was looking for a point of view. I asked him: 'To see what?' He answered: 'A point of view where I can no longer see myself.' I could have told him, but I didn't have the courage, that he could stop looking, that if that were all there was to it he need not have travelled so far. Because he would never be in his own field of view. As long as they avoid mirrors, nobody ever is. Sometimes I got the impression that though he had seen so much he couldn't see things staring him in the face. Maybe that was why he thought other people couldn't see them either, why he thought he could hide. I never said what I saw. I waited for him. I no longer know whether what I heard was real or a mixture of imaginations, mine and his, beginning with the visions he described to me. I also feared that death was the discovery that he had not yet been able to make, though he had certainly not gone out of his way to avoid it, and that this discovery was more terrible than whatever would lead to his death. What I do know is that when he left the village for the last time, he was fleeing something. And I've already said that, but I repeat it because I don't want you to forget it. At most, there was room for one single mission and one single image in his head. You will have to learn to remember him as a man outside his own field of vision, if you want to see him the way I did. It did take me a long time to understand what he meant by all this, and that was the worst part of his words: that he, unlike other people, lived outside himself. He saw himself as a foreigner and when he travelled all he wanted was to try to come back to himself, to a place where he would no longer be forced to see himself. His flight was the product of his failure. In some way, he killed himself in order to force himself out of his own field of vision, to cease to see himself.

13

Buell Quain's final departure from the village resembled a flight. His journey through the forest with the two boys he had hired to guide him to Carolina was like a struggle against time, or a flight from a pursuer. If he really was crazy, and notwithstanding the psychological cliché, it was a flight from himself, from the doppelgänger that would kill him if a new crisis caught up with him. It was indeed drawing nearer. He must have felt that something was about to happen and decided to leave before it was too late. In his loneliness, his ghosts always accompanied him. He saw himself as another, as someone he was trying to get rid of. He was dragging someone in his wake. He carried a burden: Cãmtwỳon. 'Every death is a murder,' he had written to Ruth Benedict about the Trumai. 'Imaginary attacks are common. The men press together, terrified, in the middle of the village – the most exposed place of all – and wait to be shot at by arrows coming out of the dark forest.' If we accept the explanation that he was ill, which is to say accept an exterior, more objective explanation, his burden becomes his own leprosied or syphilitic body. He simply could no longer stand the suffering of his body, racked by illness. In a letter of 2 September 1939, Fannie Dunn Quain writes to Dona Heloísa in search of an explanation for her son's suicide:

I think he was sick when he returned to the village in June, since he said that he would try to 'make it till December.' The most painful part of the whole story is that he had made it to within forty miles of the plane that would have brought him to Rio de Janeiro, where there was medical assistance that could have saved him. I think he tried for four days, trying desperately to return in the terrible heat, but that he ended up losing the battle – my heart is broken.

Perhaps because of my futile obsession with trying to learn what went on in his mind in those last hours, and my vain efforts to understand his madness, I sometimes got to thinking that he might have been fleeing not only a personal demon but something objective and concrete, someone of flesh and blood. When we met, I asked the anthropologist who had written the newspaper article if she had ever considered the possibility that he had been murdered. She rejected the suggestion out of hand. There was no possibility that he hadn't killed himself. Nothing pointed in any other direction, starting with the letters he left behind. And I knew she was right. I didn't push the point. Maybe Quain had his reasons for not letting on that he was in mortal danger. What I was suggesting made no sense; my words were contaminated by his madness. What I meant was that he might have been pushed to suicide, that he might have killed himself in a panic, once he understood that he couldn't escape not only his guilt, but also a real mortal danger. Maybe there were reasons for him to be killed. Maybe he didn't want those reasons to emerge. 'The Indians are safe, which is a source of satisfaction.' Maybe he preferred to kill himself. It all depended on what he had done in the village. For me, the answer could only be in one of the letters he wrote before he died, letters which had disappeared along with the people they were addressed to. Even so, it was improbable that – if there were a clue in one of the letters he left for his father, his brother-in-law, or the missionary Thomas Young – that explanation would never have emerged. I started to nurse the suspicion that there must have been an eighth letter.

We read poems as best we can and take from them what we wish, finding meanings that relate to our own experience. On a weekend at the beach, during a sleepless night, weeks after I started investigating the death of Quain and a mystery dormant for sixty-two years, I opened at random an anthology of Carlos Drummond de Andrade's work. There was a poem called 'Elegy 1938':

You work without joy for a fleeting world,
where shapes and actions enclose no example.
You laboriously repeat the universal gestures,
feeling cold and heat, the lack of money, hunger and
    sexual desire.
[. . .] Proud heart, hurry to confess your defeat
and postpone collective happiness to another century.
Accept rain, war, unemployment, and unjust
    distribution
because you cannot, alone, blow up the island of
    Manhattan.

14

This is for when you get here. He returned to Carolina without shoes. He wanted to spend his birthday in the city. That night, he spoke to me of another island. He said I couldn't imagine it. I had already not imagined it before, when he spoke to me of the island where he had spent ten months among the Pacific natives, four years before, on the other side of the world. Now he wanted to talk about a different island. It wasn't the island where he slept under the stars, soothed by the stories a native told him from dusk to dawn, for weeks on end. I remember seeing him laugh at his own story for the first time, when he got to Carolina, when he spoke to me of the Pacific island, the first night we drank together, more than two months before, telling me of the nudges the native gave him in a vain attempt to keep him awake, and how uncomfortable I got when he suddenly stopped laughing and adopted a serious expression for the rest of the story, telling me that the native, seeing it was pointless to try to keep him awake, ended up stretching out beside him. I feared he thought I was tired of his stories and that perhaps he was giving me a hint by relating this anecdote. When the ethnologist awoke on his Pacific island, the sun was already high and his raconteur had departed. When he returned to Carolina at the end of May, he proudly showed me a photograph and a drawing he himself had made, of enormous, powerful black men, so that I could get an idea of what he was talking about. I couldn't have imagined that the village wasn't on the beach but on a hill, until he told me about the Interior Forest, governed by a chief who kept a whale tooth hanging at his neck as a symbol of his power. On the island, the chiefs were sacred, as was everything they touched and all those who touched them. The coastal villages had been acculturated by invaders from other islands, who had themselves been influenced by the Europeans. Only the natives of the interior still maintained intact what he was looking for: a society in which, despite the rigidity of the law, individuals themselves chose their roles from within an established structure and out of a given repertory. There was a range of social options, though a restricted one, and a degree of internal mobility. That's what he told me. He was always fascinated by islands. They are isolated universes. He got his first job when he was only fifteen and went to work, during the summer holidays of 1928, as a 'controller of time and of hours' – in these awkward terms he tried to explain, with the help of gestures, his job on a railway worksite in an unexplored area in the heart of Canada. His phrase had the involuntary poetry that comes when from trying to express oneself without knowing the language. He used his days off to explore the islands of the region, sketching maps and sending them home in place of letters, showing his place in the world. He moved among boulders and fir woods, spending hours on end exploring unknown regions, acting out his fantasy of the solitary pioneer, losing himself in nature until only the limits of his own body restricted his liberty, until only his body kept him from merging with the landscape his spirit had already joined. In the Arctic summer he explored these territories alone, areas infested with mosquitoes, only charted by an irresistible combination of his experience and his imagination. Just as I am now trying to reproduce him. You will have to forgive the shortcomings of a poor backwoodsman who knows nothing of the world and has never seen snow and can no longer separate his imagination from what he really heard. But it wasn't of these islands that he spoke when he returned to Carolina, shoeless and humiliated, at the end of May. He spoke of another island, where he had arrived by boat, two hours by train from the city. An island he first visited as an adult. He spoke of a house with several rooms, all filled with friends. He no longer spoke with sadness or joy. And I can't say how he felt about that recollection. He told me about an afternoon he returned from a solitary walk on the beach. He found an exceptionally empty house and a man seated in the kitchen. Before he could introduce himself, the stranger, emerging from the darkness, took out a camera and captured for ever the fright and discomfort on the face of the anthropologist, surprised by the unknown man. On one of the nights he spent at my house, Dr Buell confessed that he had come to Brazil on a mission, to dispel the image revealed in that portrait. Like a challenge, a bet he had made with himself. He had been betrayed by the intruder and his camera. He couldn't allow that snapshot to be the most revealing image of himself. The photographer had taken him by surprise, before he could say anything. And though they later became friends, for a long time the stranger didn't succeed in taking another picture of him. Until he burst unexpectedly into his apartment one day, unannounced, after he found out Quain was leaving for Brazil. He wanted a souvenir of his friend before he departed for the South American jungle. All I know is that you are that stranger.

15

In October 1939, aged sixty-five, Fannie Quain sent three pictures of her son to Heloísa Alberto Torres. The largest had been taken in a studio in Minneapolis, before he left for Fiji. The other two portraits, one in profile and one full-face, had been taken in 1937, when Buell Quain was working in his apartment in New York. He was probably putting the final touches to the two books about Fiji that, thanks to the efforts of his mother and Ruth Benedict, would be published after his death. 'A friend, an artist from New York whose hobby was this kind of thing, made Buell promise that one day he would let him take his photograph. The friend got tired of waiting and went to Buell's apartment before he had a chance to shave or change his clothes,' wrote his mother, who was always so careful to protect her son's image. These were the pictures the ethnologist brought to Brazil and gave to people he met as souvenirs. In December 1939, on the first Christmas after Quain's death, Heloísa Alberto Torres replied to his mother, thanking her for the pictures: 'The largest one gave me a bit of a surprise. I didn't know he had such beautiful hair, since he cut it so short when he came to Brazil. But his expression, though sad, is excellent, that one he had when he was lost in thought.' The two women seem to have tacitly and mutually encouraged this kind of self-deluding dialogue. Something made me think they both knew something they were pretending not to know. In the same letter, however, perhaps to calm the anxious mother, Dona Heloísa says things that at the very least contradict a strange letter she had sent Quain himself a few months before his suicide.

Dona Heloísa wrote to the ethnologist's mother: 'He seemed so happy, in such a good mood, when he left Rio.' She went on to say that his Columbia colleagues were equally surprised by his breakdown.

Several other sources give the lie to this statement. For example: in a letter of 12 March 1939, Ruth Landes writes to Ruth Benedict: 'Buell left for the north about a week ago. He seemed healthy, but right before he left he started behaving very nervously.' When, five months later, Quain kills himself, Benedict, worried about the effect of the news on Charles Wagley, isolated among the Tapirapé, in Mato Grosso, asks his 'good friend' Carl Withers to send him an encouraging letter. Withers answers Benedict: 'I was very touched by the care you took to keep Chuck from being too shocked by poor Buell's death. But just between us, judging by the letters he sent me from Rio, I don't think he would have been terribly surprised.'

But the most perturbing contradictory evidence of the sunny image Dona Heloísa tried to communicate to Quain's mother about her son's last days in Rio de Janeiro, if only just to try to comfort her, is an enigmatic letter she herself sent the ethnologist, in English, on 7 May 1939. He was

still among the Krahô. The pretext was an offer of future
employment as a professor at the National Museum:

I wonder what led you to scratch out the last part
of your letter. Before the opportunity comes up to think
about your staying in Brazil, I'd like us to have a serious
conversation. I'm afraid it can't wait long and I ask you
to let me speak *à cœur ouvert*. I'm sure you won't be
aggrieved by anything I write. I need to be able to have
full confidence in you and I resent certain things that
I know you were doing in Rio. I often wanted to talk
to you about this. Maybe I could have helped you. I'm
sure you know what I'm talking about. Besides, you
shouldn't forget that, if something happens in the village
or even in civilized towns, the [Indian Protection] Service
would find out about it, and there would be complaints
about my friends. You can be sure that I would be the
first to suffer any consequences. Buell, I know that
you're not going to take rum to the village. I know that
you are not going to drink too much when you're in
Carolina. I know you're not going to touch the Indian
women. Write and tell me that I can count on you. I
must confess that sometimes you scare me; I think you
are very unstable, and I fear for your future. I would
have liked you to talk to me more and tell me about
what you were doing. I hope your stay in Brazil does
you good, and I think that the longer you stay the better.
I will be very happy to help you and I want you to be
sure that your old friend has much more understanding

for human misery than she might appear to. I wonder
if you are going to understand exactly what I'm trying
to say, but I hope that your intelligence and sensitivity
will supplement my meagre powers of expression in your
language.

For a while, I scratched my head trying to work out
what she was really saying in that letter, and what she
meant by 'human misery'. It was code for something only
Quain could know.

On 27 May, during his visit to Carolina, after seeing
the letter, Quain replied to Dona Heloísa: 'You are right
to ask me to be careful of my reputation. But you can be
sure that my sex life is impeccable and that I have no more
than an occasional drink. I can't work and drink at the
same time.'

On 4 July, less than a month before his suicide, he
wrote Margaret Mead an abruptly interrupted letter, which
he didn't post: 'I doubt that anywhere else in the world
contains such pure indigenous cultures. But despite all
the virtues of the Xingu, I'd like to leave Brazil once and
for all and limit my work to regions . . .'

In the same letter, found among the belongings the
Krahô brought to Carolina, Quain complained of the difficulties of working with the Indians in Brazil:

I think it might be attributed to the undisciplined, spine-
less Brazilian culture itself. My Indians are used to
dealing with the kind of degenerate rural Brazilian that

has set himself up around here – it is marginal land, and the trash of Brazil lives here. Both the Brazilians and the Indians I've seen are spoiled children who sob if they don't get what they want, and who never keep their promises, as soon as you turn your back. The climate is anarchic and not at all pleasant. The society seems to have frayed. My difficulties here can in large part be attributed to the Brazilian influence. Brazil, in turn, surely absorbed many of the most distasteful characteristics of the indigenous cultures with which it had initial contact. An engineer from Carolina goes into the water to bathe with the same peculiar gesture as the Krahô, and the Indians of the Xingu. Nobody in Rio de Janeiro obeys the no-smoking signs, because 'in Brazil we don't pay much attention to that kind of rule.' Brazilian children always ask travelers for a 'blessing.' The habit might not be indigenous in origin, but it meshes perfectly with the Indians' temperament. The Brazilians are happy to ask for things at random.

Quain, on the other hand, never planned to leave his destiny to chance. Not even in the hour of his death.

This was what he saw. He arrived in Rio de Janeiro just before Carnival began and stayed in a boarding house on the Rua do Riachuelo, in Lapa. The neighbourhood was known for its 'cheap love hotels', in the words of Luís Martins, the celebrated chronicler of Rio's prostitutes and lowlifes. At the bottom of a letter of introduction signed by Franz Boas, the young ethnologist wrote his new address in Rio: 'B. H. Quain, 107 Rua Riachuelo (Pensão Gustavo)'. At this time, *Banana da terra*, the film that immortalized Carmen Miranda wearing bananas on her head while singing 'O que é que a baiana tem?', premiered in the Metro-Passeio cinema, in downtown Rio. The film inspired the Carnival merrymakers, who spread out through the streets of Lapa in groups, cross-dressed as *baianas*, their heads covered with fruit. At that same Carnival of 1938, one of the leading figures of local myth, an icon of the area's mischief-making, crime, and homosexuality, won the dance contest at the Teatro República, near the Praça Tiradentes. His sequined costume was inspired by the bats of the north-east, his native region. From then on he was known as Madame Sin, in homage to Cecil B. DeMille's film of the same name.

16

This is for when you get here. I know what he told me and what I imagined. You know about things from that island that I myself can never know. That's the only reason I'm taking the trouble to write down what I do know. If the things I have to say are only halfway complete, and if they sound trivial to anyone else, it's because they're waiting for you to fill in the rest of their meaning. You're the only one who can understand what I mean, because you have the key I lack. You're the only one who knows the other part of the story. I've waited for several years, but I can no longer trust to luck. I too would have a lot of questions for you. About his memories of that island two hours outside the city, for example. He told me about the beach house and I tried to imagine it, and I saw a glass-and-wood construction facing the sea between the dunes and two figures in an attic at the close of a rainy afternoon, after the revelation that for ever changed both their lives. Only you can know what I'm talking about. It can only have been at the beach house where he spoke to you about her for the first time. If not, then why, on one of the nights he came looking for me in Carolina, drunk, would he have associated the rain and the sea with the disappointment he inflicted on those who loved him? You must have talked about that woman. He thought you didn't know about her. And that was when the betrayal was revealed. On that rainy night you told him not only that you knew everything, but that you were involved with her too. And for her it was a shock whose consequences you couldn't imagine. I truly believe that nothing can surprise a person who can hear his own voice in other people. He spoke to me of you without telling me your name. He spoke of the man who had betrayed him. But, if this is any help to you, he also recognized your friendship. Ultimately, what he referred to as betrayal were his own actions. You should know that he somehow recognized that he had betrayed you too.

The roles were reversed: unlike the black man who had sung songs to him on a Pacific island until he fell asleep, and who was no longer at his side when he woke up at sunrise, you were the one who woke up alone the next morning, when he unexpectedly left the beach house for the last time. The two figures had talked about a woman on a rainy night. What he hadn't known until then was that you too were involved with her. I can guess at your reasons. You thought that that way he'd leave her. You didn't want to lose him. And he vanished. When you got up, the house was empty. Maybe you already suspected that if you didn't go looking for him you would never see him again, but you had to get the news from mutual friends, to discover that he was leaving for Brazil. He must have been planning the trip for months, in silence, only making up his mind after that rainy night on the beach. Anyway, you had to understand that the conversation had been a farewell, in his way. That is why you ran to Dr Buell's house in the city, determined to take

*the pictures that would be your only souvenir of him, the
trace he left of his brief passage on the earth.*

*When, in his haziest, most melancholy moments, he spoke
of the woman, without specifying whether it was his own
wife, I always associated her with the woman you talked
about at the beach house, the one that brought an end to
your friendship. I could only guess. He mentioned a woman,
a man who betrayed him, and nobody else, if you want to
know. At first, I thought it had to be his wife, the same one
he mentioned to the Indians before killing himself. The
woman who betrayed him and who disobeyed him by accept-
ing a job at a North American newspaper. The strange thing
is that he told me right after we met that he wasn't married.
I got to thinking that he might have been talking about his
own wife when he spoke of that woman, but only until he
told me about a night in the city when, on his way back
home – he actually mentioned returning to a hotel rather
than to a house – the woman he was with was suddenly
perturbed by the sight of a tiny young woman on the train.
He couldn't even identify the girl among all the other passengers. But the woman was so upset that they had to get out
four stations before the hotel and walk the rest of the way.
She was as rattled as if she had seen a ghost. And no matter
how much he asked, she wouldn't tell him why. Days later,
when she awoke from a nightmare screaming the name of a
girl she hadn't seen in the last three years and who, by an
unhappy coincidence, had reappeared as a spectre in the
same train carriage as she and Dr Buell, only then, in bed,
when he had calmed her down, was she forced to tell him*

what had made her rush from that train. The story went back to the time before they had met, she and Dr Buell. The girl in the train was an odd little person, with an odd name, he recalled. She had come to New York from the South, planning to study and make a career for herself in the music world. Inadvertently, she had found lodgings in a brothel, and in her utter ingenuousness she thanked her lucky stars for having been accepted at a young ladies' boarding house. And that is where the two of them met, the newly arrived Southerner and the old hand, the woman whom, among the Indians, he would refer to as his wife, shortly before his death. Seeing the Southern girl's innocence, she offered to guide her to the subway she needed to take to her music school and to keep an eye on her money. One need hardly add that before the girl knew what hit her, her buddy from the boarding house had disappeared with all her savings, just as she realized that her ladies' hotel was really a brothel. The two never met again. The woman Dr Buell called his wife could never have imagined that she would come across her again in another huge city, until she saw her on the train, like a phantom, among the other passengers. The story was left unfinished and was apparently inconsequential, but he narrated it carefully, as he tended to do when he had something important to reveal. I understood what he was trying to tell me. He wanted to make it clear to me that he carried on with prostitutes.

Everything he told me was ambiguous. I knew about the scar on his belly that very first night. He only revealed it to the Indians in the desperate hours before his death, when he had other surprises for them as well. It's strange that they had never seen it before, since they must often have bathed together. He told them it was the result of a long-ago illness, an illness that returned as a fever. Since this time the fever hadn't come, it was a sign that his days were numbered. He chose to stay one step ahead of the suffering of that unavoidable death. On the first night he came to my house in Carolina, in March, he compulsively, thoughtlessly, lifted up his shirt to show me the scar. He was talking about the Trumai when he mentioned offhand that his father was a surgeon. He never said it in so many words, but I understood, horrified, that in childhood my friend had been operated on by his own father.

We agreed that I would accompany him on horseback for the first day of his trip back to the village. The journey was tiring, and I did what I could to help him. I offered to stay with him during the whole first part of the trip, an entire day on the backs of the animals. We spent the night in the forest. We talked the whole night. Maybe he already knew, or could guess, what was about to happen. Maybe he was trying to fool himself. The Indians knew a well-watered place where we could spend the night. At the end of the first day, they cut palm fronds, built a thatched hut as shelter, and made a fire. After the evening meal, they went to sleep, and the two of us stayed up talking. The sky was covered with stars. He told me about several of them, the things he had heard about them in Fiji. Stars have no importance. The Indians believed that stars are bonfires. They are lit at night by the villagers and Indians who were trapped in the sky *when the staircase that linked the celestial sphere to the Earth was removed. And they have remained there, in the other world that covers us like a hat or like a mirror. It doesn't matter what the stars mean to us, to the Indians, or to the Pacific natives. On that night, he drank too much. He got drunk very quickly. I don't doubt that he was weaker and had less resistance to alcohol. He had already been drinking on the journey. Against my wishes, he had brought rum with him. Towards the end of the afternoon, he lashed out at the Indians, who hadn't managed to make up the hut the way he wanted it. It began as soon as he saw them emerging from the forest with palm fronds, which seemed inadequate to him. Nobody understood him. He must have been speaking in English, forgetting where he was. I watched it all in silence. He jerked the piece of luggage where he had hidden the* cachaça *from the hands of one of the Indians, while the poor Krahô was trying to place it at the foot of an* embaré *tree, the same baggage he had handed to the man hours before, when he could no longer carry it. I had never seen him like that. The Indians crouched down. He yelled at them until he suddenly went quiet, as if snapping out of a profound sleep and awakening in a daze. He shut up and left for the water. When he came back, we were all sitting around the fire. He was calmer. He ate in silence and as soon as the Indians went to sleep he apologized. But that was it. As if nothing had happened, he started to talk about the land-scape of the place he came from, in the United States, which sometimes resembled the low scrubby plains that surrounded us. He kept drinking while sitting in front of the fire. He* told me that Dona Heloísa had prohibited him from bringing drink to the village and that that was why we needed to finish it there and then. He tried to smile. I took a few swallows, just to be polite. He told me he was waiting for a very important letter from the United States and he made me promise that as soon as the Condor plane arrived in Carolina, I would forward any correspondence to the village with a porter. I promised that I would send my own brother on horseback. I didn't know, as I've said, that those last letters contained a death sentence. He told me a story that his father, the surgeon, had told him when they went to Europe for the first time, when he was still a teenager. There was a ghost ship, wandering the seas since time immemorial, that never managed to put into port. Every time it crossed the path of another ship, the members of its crew approached in small boats to beg the sailors of the other vessel to take bundles of letters back to dry land. When they got into port, though, the sailors always discovered that the letters were addressed to people nobody knew of or who had died long before. Dr Buell also told me about the time he was wandering through Rio de Janeiro and saw, between Lapa and Catete, a columned temple. A phrase was inscribed at the entrance: 'The living are always, and increasingly, necessarily governed by the dead'. He asked me if I had ever thought of that, if I had any notion of what it meant. He asked if I had ever been in Rio de Janeiro during Carnival. He was getting drunker and drunker. I was no longer sober myself. I don't remember everything I heard. I imagined his dreams and his nightmares. He told me that he reached Rio during the Carnival of 1938, and *that he had met a tall, striking black woman, dressed up as a nurse, at a street party. She was wearing a white uniform, a white hat, and white shoes, which set off her tar-coloured skin, shimmering with sweat. He could hardly speak Portuguese. He didn't understand a word she was saying. He was drunk. He took her to his boarding house room, they slept together, but when he woke up the next morning she was gone, like the storyteller of Fiji, who abandoned him before sunrise, and in place of the nurse there was a man in his bed, a strong, naked black man, like the native in the pictures he showed me. He no longer had any idea what had happened, or how that man had got there. He stammered out denials.*

This is for when you get here. Among the songs, legends, and stories that the black man told him beneath the stars of his Pacific island, on the other side of the world, there was one that Dr Buell saved to tell me on the night we went our separate ways. It was the story of a chief from Vanua Levu who, on the night before a visit to another village, heard about a man who had been seducing all the women who passed that way. Intending to play a trick on him, he begged his ancestors to lend him the appearance of a woman before he reached the village. He entered the river and an eel turned him into a girl. He went to the village and the seducer approached him as soon as he arrived. He invited him to sleep under the same roof. The chief rejected all his approaches and proposals, until the seducer, annoyed and with no other strategy to fall back on, ended up proposing marriage. On the following day, while the chief pretended to be getting dressed, the man came to seduce her once more. This time the chief put up no resistance. When the seducer lay on top of him, the two erect penises touched and the seducer fled in shame, pursued by the chief, who now demanded that they sleep together. At the end of the story, Dr Buell turned to me, smiled, and said he was very sick. After that he mumbled something under his breath that I understood as: 'Every death is a murder.' I still didn't know what he could mean by that, and at that point he fell asleep, as if in a faint. I too slept heavily that night. So much so that when I got up the next day, unsure of what I had heard or whether he had meant it seriously, Dr Buell and the Indians were already getting ready to leave. They were having their coffee. He had decided to tell me everything on the last night, between one drink and another, on his way to the village, while the Indians were asleep. It was his legacy for my journey, to ponder over when I was alone with the horses. He and the Indians would continue on foot and I would return to Carolina by myself, taking what he had told me and letting it echo inside my head. When I saw him leave with the Indians that morning, turning and waving for the last time before disappearing into the bush, I didn't want to imagine, though for a moment the thought crossed my mind, that that was our farewell.

17

In February 1939, aged thirty-seven, the French-Swiss anthropologist Alfred Métraux, a Latin American specialist, met Charles Wagley on board a boat from New York to Rio de Janeiro. In Barbados, the two got to know each other as they strolled through Bridgetown. On their way back to the ship and the sea, Wagley told Métraux the story of his life. He had a developmentally impaired brother. The fifteen-year-old boy had an eleven-year-old's body. Wagley had decided to dedicate part of his savings to an attempt to cure his adored younger brother. He didn't, however, seem to like his mother. He said that she had been a cabaret dancer, a private tutor, and that she worked in a restaurant. He said he didn't feel comfortable with her lack of education. The confession moved the Swiss anthropologist, who until that point had bemoaned the 'tiresome simplicity' of his young American colleague. 'I was also impressed by the casual manner he spoke of pederasty. He himself confirmed the impression I had of the subject. He told me of his amorous successes: another insight into the depths of American life,' he wrote in his diary.

Upon arriving in Rio, on 9 February, Métraux paid a visit to Heloísa Alberto Torres in her office in the Empress's Chapel in the National Museum. The building was crumbling. In his notes, the Swiss anthropologist tells of his meeting with a mysterious man named 'Cowan', of whom there is no mention in any other place: 'An energetic face, regular, well-defined features, slightly eager, broad shoulders.'

Back in the Hotel Belvedere, in Copacabana, Métraux had dinner with an American woman who had arrived on the same ship and with whom he had been flirting for several days. Wagley and 'Cowan' joined them. It is in this passage of the diary that the identity of the mysterious character is finally revealed, by deduction: 'Cowan told of his journey to the Xingu, and then brought the conversation around to the subject of his syphilis. In the brutal frankness of his talk, in the jokes he made about his condition, I thought I could make out a desperate bravado. Cowan is very drunk and fills the room with his booming voice. Wagley calms him with a delicate, friendly "psit, psits".' It becomes obvious that the Swiss anthropologist hadn't registered the young American ethnologist's name when he was introduced to Quain. Quain, Cowan. At dinner the following night, Wagley seems very depressed.

In 1947, on another trip to Rio, Métraux dined with Bernard Mishkin, a young Columbia anthropologist, whom he found bitter, pretentious, and gossipy. Mishkin took advantage of the occasion to tell him of Wagley's youth: 'Divorced mother, a poor and neglected childhood.' Then he passes some information about Quain, who had been dead for eight years: 'Son of a wealthy alcoholic father and a neurotic, dominating mother. Forced himself into homosexuality with blacks, of whom he has a horror. Talented guy, a poet.' Métraux couldn't contain himself in his notes: 'As a calumniator, nobody outdoes Mishkin.'

18

What he meant to say was something else. I don't know if you realize the implications of the things he told me, or what kind of reaction they could have sparked if they had reached the ears of the authorities. They would think the worst. Everything would lead them to conclude that he had committed acts in the village, acts contrary to human nature, that would justify the Indians in killing him. The easiest thing to do would be to attack the Indians. You can't imagine the responsibility he placed on my shoulders. Indirectly, he charged me with making sure the letters, the ones he wrote just before dying, reached their addressees, like the sailors who took letters to the dead back to dry land. But he couldn't imagine how frightened I was. He couldn't imagine that, out of fear, I would end up keeping one of the letters rather than taking a chance on sending it. Out of pure mistrust. What he told me, so coolly, there in front of the fire, between one story and the next, made the Indians suspects in a crime of vengeance or self-defence. You can't imagine how it was back then, or how this country still is, an absurd world driven by mistrust. Try to forgive me. Everything led me to believe that the letter he left upon his death could reveal the truth, whatever it was. Truth and lies do not have the same meanings they had before they arrived here. And I couldn't take the risk. It was the only thing I couldn't allow to emerge. If the

Indians were so afraid of being accused of something, it certainly wasn't because they had killed him but because they might have had reason to. Although they had done nothing and he had been rather emphatic, and generous, in making that clear. He killed himself so that there would be no doubts about his death. And to absolve them, because his existence alone – and his presence in the village – was enough to incriminate them. That is what finally dawned on him in his madness. Among the letters he left, the only ones that were sealed were the ones to his father, his brother-in-law, and you. The others do not only absolve the Indians, they excuse the ethnologist from his own guilt and place him above suspicion. Suicide eliminates the possibility of homicide as well as cancelling out the motives of anyone who might have had reason to kill him, a father or a mother avenging a son, a husband avenging a wife, siblings avenging a sibling. They all end up above suspicion. They are all innocent. I am sure that what he told me slowly, on those nine nights, was a confession, but of something more than what he seemed to be confessing. It was the preparation for his death. I don't think he had done anything. What he wanted to tell me is what he could do, and that he could no longer control himself. He was always very ambiguous. I had no other choice. I decided to write an ending to this letter that belongs to you and whose contents I cannot read, partly out of ignorance, partly out of caution (I can't ask anyone to translate it), and which I have kept with the single goal of protecting them, him and the Indians, making sure it reaches its proper address. I can only hand it over personally. It was his legacy to me. I have been under suspicion ever since they fired me from my job as the head of the Manoel da Nóbrega Indian Liaison Post. Since then I've been waiting for you, but I can't take any chances. I feared that, in his madness, he might have used the sealed letter he sent you to reveal what I came to suspect at the end of those nine nights, a suspicion that only increased when I heard the news of his death: that he had beaten the murderers to it, that he no longer wanted to leave anything to chance. It took me a while to believe that he was really dead, just as it must have taken you. For a few days I thought I would still see him, that he had fled, changed his identity. Until I understood. That was when I began to fear that in his madness he might have revealed something in that letter, something that might raise suspicions. Things he wouldn't tell his father or his brother-in-law but would only tell you, whoever you are. Things that belonged not to reality, but to his madness. Things he hadn't actually done but that he feared he could no longer avoid.

This is for when you get here. You need to be ready. When you feel alone and abandoned, when you think you've lost everything, think about Dr Buell, my friend. At some point, we all feel alone and abandoned. Only ceaselessly testing the limits of our body helps us realize that we are still alive. It is not some futile whimsy, some desire to find out how far we can go, to defy our limits – though others may think we are committing acts against nature. And often enough, when we do discover what we are doing, it is too late. On his twenty-seventh birthday, he told me that he knew what death was: an excess that finally goes too far. It's getting more tired than fatigue allows, exceeding one's own capacities, reducing oneself to less than zero, using up the twenty-four hours in one day without making it to the next. What was hellish in his case was that there was no one around to help him when he reached that critical hour. When he understood that he had to go back, that he had gone too far, he no longer had the strength for the journey. Any creature, even a creeping snake, a slug, a snail, even if it's only once in its life, when it looks at a tree or a stone or a piece of the sky, sees the totality of the universe and understands for one moment what it is, where it is, what is happening around it. After his death, I sought out that tree, trying to understand. The Indians led me to the grave, covered with palm fronds. It could have been any tree. I had to believe that it had happened there. I could only find proof if I dug up the cadaver with my own hands. There are many things you can't dig up again. By myself, I didn't have the strength.

We are all dogs by the side of the road, taken by surprise, not understanding that it is always the wrong time to cross. His own self took him by surprise. I would have done anything to save him, if I had understood that he was already at the end of his strength when he went back to the village for the last time. Now I understand all the hints he was giving me, and I understand his character, his responsibilities. I would have tried to stop him. But what happened then left me paralysed, and this was, deep down, out of respect for Dr Buell. He was a proud man and I knew he would go all the way to the end. But I couldn't interfere, even less so after our last conversation, on that final night in the forest. Perhaps

*because I had already realized how unstable he was, I decided
to accompany him on horseback for the first part of the
journey – but no further – when he told me something that
today I wish I hadn't heard, since it only makes me regret
things all the more, since it only makes me all the sorrier
that I let him leave. Try to understand me. My knowledge
of his mental state was exactly what prevented me from inter-
vening. Any action on my part would have been taken as an
offence and a betrayal. It would have almost been like
breathing life into the murderous ghost that haunted him.
What he told me was for me to keep to myself, as if I had
never heard it. And that is what I did. It was my legacy from
him. Try to understand and forgive me, just as I understood
that you could never have imagined the impact your last
letter would have on a man that alone and helpless.*

*What I'm telling you is a combination of what he told me
and what I have imagined. And so in the same way, I'll let
you imagine everything I can't bring myself to tell you.*

Nobody ever asked me. Manoel Perna, the Carolina engineer and former head of the Manoel da Nóbrega Indian
Liaison Post, died in 1946, drowned in the Rio Tocantins,
during a storm, while trying to rescue his little granddaughter. The Estado Novo and the war were over. He
left seven children, three boys and four girls. He was
returning to Carolina from Miracema do Tocantins. I
heard the story from his two eldest children, who promised me that he left no writings or will, not a word about
Buell Quain. Francisco Perna, from Miracema, said that
his father 'was coming back down the river to Carolina,
there was a storm, and his boat overturned. He already
had an intestinal illness. His heart couldn't take it. He
tried to paddle over and save his granddaughter, who was
clinging to a suitcase, but his body sank. The granddaughter was saved by a friend who managed to make it
to the riverbank.' It wasn't for several days after the accident that his children discovered what happened to their
father's body. Swept away by the current, it was found
and buried at some point downstream, but they never
knew exactly where. He was buried and forgotten just
like Buell Quain, in the middle of the forest. Francisco
was a boy when the anthropologist came to his father's
house: 'He was tall, red, and very nice. He was a friend

of my father's. He was very calm and polite. His suicide was a surprise.' The eldest daughter, Raimunda Perna Coelho, also remembered the ethnologist's visits to her father in Carolina: 'They talked a lot. Or went horseriding.' Today, like her brother Francisco, Raimunda lives in Miracema. I asked her what she knew about the death of Quain: 'He no longer wanted to eat after he got those last letters from home. And he said to the Indians that he had been abandoned by his wife, that she had betrayed him with his brother-in-law. That she had disobeyed him, going to work for a North American newspaper. Before he died, in order to write his last letters, he burned everything, clothes, papers, since there was no light. That was what people said in Carolina.' At the end of the day, I thought, while I was speaking with her on the phone, it was certainly possible that his brother-in-law's 'betrayal' had something to do with money. The subject recurred in all the letters he left: instructions for dispersing his belongings among Ruth Benedict and his family; for paying whatever he owed in Carolina or to the National Museum; and for the money he had promised to the Indians, especially the two who had accompanied him on his final journey. The ethnologist even attributed his suicide to family troubles. In that case, it was possible that, in his disturbed state of mind, he might have imagined that his brother-in-law 'betrayed' him by leaving his sister and niece in a vulnerable financial situation. Marion Kaiser, with a hint of wounded pride, denied any such difficulties in the letter she wrote to Ruth Benedict after her brother's suicide. Manoel Perna left no will, and I imagined the eighth letter.

Nobody ever asked me. And so I never needed to answer. My father died over eleven years ago, on the eve of the war that preceded the current one and in many ways foreshadowed it. Today, wars are constant. I wasn't living in Brazil. My sister called me, telling me to prepare for the worst. The story isn't simple. At a certain point, my father started having trouble walking. Since he had always been a heavy drinker – so much that he occasionally even took a glass of whisky with him when he went out driving by himself – we thought it was the cumulative effect of alcohol. That's when he started having trouble expressing himself. He couldn't speak clearly; he tripped over his tongue. He forgot to sign cheques. He lived with a Lebanese woman he had met at the swimming pool of his apartment building, in São Conrado. My father had several women, sometimes simultaneously. He liked having lovers, and he liked them to be a bit sleazy. And though he was not a liberal man, I always thought that deep down he had some kind of understanding for and sympathy with people who let themselves be carried away by desire, down paths they cannot choose, paths which often lead to their own destruction. When I was little, he once said, suddenly and for no apparent reason, except possibly a fabulous intuition or a magical foresight (neither of which he possessed), that 'men don't love by themselves, without women'. He could only be referring to his own experience,

I thought. The comment may have been provoked by his seeing me masturbating beneath the sheets while I pretended to be asleep. At that time I had absolutely no self-control. It was on one of those nights when we shared a cheap hotel room in some city in the interior of Mato Grosso – Barra do Garças, if I'm not mistaken – on our way out to the ranches. In that single case, I can believe that the comment was not meant to sound repressive, but came from some protective feeling of foresight. He was speaking of something he knew from his own experience. He had given himself over to a desire that, if it had a sadistic side, also had its share of masochism. It might seem simplistic, but what he took from women in his younger years he had to pay back to the women who surrounded him in his old age. I never really found out what the story was about him and the cousin he had been living with for years and who had invested a considerable sum in his jungle livestock ranches. He apparently started taking her money at the same time that he began to be seen with a woman twenty years younger, some sort of beauty queen, whom he must have met in one of those 'singles' or 'executive' bars. He made no effort to conceal the relationship or to avoid humiliating his cousin (to the contrary, it all seemed to be well thought-out). On one of his trips to Rio, he and this beauty queen took me, for the first time in my life and without telling me where we were going, to a place where Afro-Brazilian rituals were performed. They were terrifying to a child. At the same time he couldn't resist the appeal of a whore, he needed to make the woman he was living with feel like one. My father spent a weekend with the beauty queen at the beach house he and his cousin owned. Her friends saw him with the girl. It was a scandal. The cousin called in her lawyers to reclaim the money she'd lost to my father. Nobody could reclaim for her the pride with which she had defied her brother years before, when he warned her about her cousin, and when she decided, flying in the face of all good sense, to move in with him, because she was in love. Her brother had cut her off. Time proved him right. My father had a reputation. He went overboard in his perversion, which was something between sadism and masochism, when he, always attracted by the lower orders, got involved with people even worse than he was. He went from villain to victim, from sadist to masochist. That was the risk he'd taken from the beginning, and that's when he started having to pay. There was one woman he lived with for several years. To his surprise, when my father began playing the traditional last scene of his sadistic act, she revealed that she wasn't only a whore in bed and released to all of São Paulo a letter outlining all the financial shenanigans of the lover who was now trying to dump her penniless on the street. I don't know if that was the main reason, but the fact is that he decided to leave Brazil. He took advantage of a stopover in Rio, appeared at my mother's house with the disillusioned air of someone who has just taken a thrashing, and spent the afternoon talking to us, and to her, which he hadn't done in years and which shocked me. In the United States, he ended up getting married again, which, for a man of his age and personal history, was either naive or accidental. This time it was to a Cuban bank employee who was responsible for his account and knew of every penny he had. For me, that was the last step, a clear sign that the balance of his perversity had been lost with age. Without even noticing, he had fallen into a trap, out of his own desire. Not that the Cuban didn't suffer at his hands too. To give an example, my father bought a thirty-odd-foot sailing boat and forced his wife – who didn't know how to swim – to go with him – who didn't know how to sail – and an old retired sailor on night trips between Florida and the Bahamas. One day they were caught by an unexpected storm and all three barely escaped alive. At that point the excursions ceased. When I visited them in Treasure Cay, a remote island in the Bahamas, the boat no longer left its anchorage and the tortures he inflicted on his wife were limited to fighting and sex, which, he later told me, she really didn't enjoy, at least with him. When everything started falling apart, the two of them moved to Rio. When my father began to push her, she flew back to Miami, filed for divorce, and demanded half his property. No other woman had ever dared do that to him. He was taken by surprise. To make things worse, he had placed everything he owned in the United States (an apartment, a boat, and two cars), as well as his investments, in her name. It was to do with taxes and his kind of residential visa. To avoid losing half of what he had in Brazil, his Brazilian lawyer advised him not to show up for the hearing in Miami and to let her keep the American property. And my father never again set foot in the United States. Alone in Rio, he started drinking and taking anti-depressants and tranquillizers at the same time. One day, after six months of not speaking to me, because he disapproved of my lifestyle (he wanted me to work, like him, instead of finishing college), he called me and asked for help. He didn't know where he was (he was at home), he didn't know where his wife was (she had left him and gone back to the United States), he didn't know who he was (he was my father). He started going out with more than one woman a week, and he occasionally introduced them to me, with pride. He spent what he didn't have and spent his nights like a twenty-year-old playboy. He was over sixty. One day he met a neighbour from his building, a Lebanese woman, and then things seemed to be settling down. But instead he started to deteriorate. He kicked her out of his apartment and she came back a week later. He kicked her out again and she came back, and that was how she managed to impose herself on him, and he couldn't really resist. She started taking over everything that belonged to him, and by the time my sister and I realized it, it was already too late. My father could no longer speak or walk and the Lebanese woman had managed to get a power of attorney that allowed him to sign with thumbprints instead of in writing. For a while, nobody knew what was the matter with him. They ran a lot of tests and couldn't find anything. Finally a doctor requested a brain scan and discovered that he had spongy matter in his brain. It was strong evidence that my father had Creutzfeldt–Jakob syndrome, an extremely rare and fatal disease. His brain was turning into a sponge. We decided that we needed to place him in a home, for reasons both practical and objective. That was when we happened upon the power of attorney, which the Lebanese woman had failed to mention. And one thing led to another. We discovered that she had tracked down my father's lawyer in São Paulo, through the list of properties he still possessed. She had already placed the apartment in Rio in her name. She had got her hands on his stock certificates and everything else that he kept in a safe that, in principle, only he and I had access to. She had cleaned out all his bank accounts and investments. When we asked her for an explanation, she prohibited us, in her gravelly voice, from entering the apartment or the building. She was acting under her lawyer's instructions. The scene was Dantesque. When we confronted her, she started screaming. My father was in bed, watching everything with wide eyes, mute and motionless. She screamed that we were trying to rob him, that we were there to rob him. I don't know how much he could still understand. In a superhuman effort, he looked at me and managed to stammer, more than once, a single word: 'Shameless!' It was the last thing I heard my father say that made any sense. My sister and I sued for an injunction. It all took months. Meanwhile, I was offered a job in Paris. It was a unique opportunity that I couldn't turn down. I left while the suit was still under way. Three months later, my sister called me to tell me to prepare for the worst. The worst was having to force entry into his apartment (with a court order), accompanied by a court officer (and, if necessary, the police), a doctor, and two nurses, to take my father from his bed against his will (if he still had one – there was no way to know), put him in an ambulance and take him to São Paulo immediately. I arrived in Rio on a direct flight from Paris. I had dinner with my sister and a doctor who was a friend of hers who had planned the whole thing. He would be admitted to a none too reputable hospital in São Paulo, the only one that would accept him in that state, and the next morning we went with the ambulance and the court officer to the building in São Conrado. The Lebanese woman had been tipped off and knew what was going to happen. She was waiting for us with her son and a lawyer. When we took my father out of the apartment, she still tried to scream and cry, but just as she was about to start a scene, she was inter-rupted by her son and the lawyer, who convinced her that it wouldn't help, it would only make things worse, and she didn't let out another peep. I don't know how much my father understood. The expression in his eyes could have been incomprehension or fear. Sometimes I don't know what I did, and I'm not sure if I regret it. I don't know who was right. And what if before he lost conscious-ness, if he really did lose it, my father had decided to die next to that woman, in that apartment? If he had decided to give everything he had to her? We spent five hours in the ambulance before we got to São Paulo. My sister and I travelled beside him. I tried to calm him down, telling him that everything would turn out fine, but I heard the falseness of my own words as he looked at me, immobile, with a piercing look, whether of incomprehension or resigned reproach I couldn't know. He must have been able to see in my eyes what I was really saying: that nothing was going to turn out all right, nothing could turn out all right. When we reached the hospital, the doctor, my sister's friend, was waiting for us. My father was taken to a double room, in the emergency ward. It was a semi-intensive care unit. It was a miracle that they had accepted him. The guy in the other bed was already dying. The doctor had omitted to mention my father's diagnosis in order to get him in. Nobody knew what, or how contagious, his disease was. Nobody would have risked admitting him, especially because there was nothing he could do apart from wait around for death, and that wait could last months. They didn't know what caused his disease and they couldn't rule out the possibility that it was hereditary, in which case my sister and I might also have a similar end to look forward to. This was just before the mad-cow crisis erupted in England. That turned out to be a variant of Creutzfeldt–Jakob, at least in its effects and symptoms, though its level of contagion was completely different. It was before they started to suspect that a variant of the disease could be caused by the consumption of meat contaminated by a dysfunctional protein. On that very first night, the nurses began to suspect that something wasn't quite right, because of the nature of the disease and the absence of any diagnosis. They avoided being close to my father or took major precautions every time they came into the room. I had come from Paris especially for the rescue operation and had a return flight three days later. My sister and I agreed that I would spend the first three nights in the hospital and that she would come during the day. Since the other patient in the room was a solitary type who rarely received visitors, they let me spend the three nights on a small sofa next to my father. The air at night was unbreathable. There was a sharp smell in the room, which the nurses diagnosed as coming from an infection in my father's mouth. None of the medicine they gave him helped. His death would be ghastly, as his organs and functions failed one by one, three months after he arrived at the hospital. The nurses saw what he had to look forward to. But I didn't have any idea. My sister shouldered, alone, the responsibility and the emotional burden of those months of waiting. When she finally called to tell me he had died, the night before the funeral, she told me that in his last hours he had cried tears of blood. And I tried not to imagine it. I didn't go back for the funeral.

I hardly slept the first night. My father's suffering wouldn't allow me to sleep. His breathing was laboured, he moaned every once in a while, he wanted to say something. I tried to calm him down, in vain. When we had arrived, the curtains around the other bed were drawn. In the middle of the night, the other patient also started to mumble. Every once in a while the nurse would come and give him an injection. I didn't see him until the morning. He had completely white hair, watery blue eyes, and was very thin. Around ten in the morning, a young man came into the room, said hello to me, greeted the old man, pulled up a chair, sat at the foot of the bed, took a book out of a bag and started reading. He read in English. To my astonishment, I immediately recognized the first lines of 'The Secret Sharer' by Joseph Conrad, one of my favourite stories from adolescence. The man had no accent. Either in Portuguese or in English. He was completely bilingual. He talked like an American from the Midwest. 'I was in time to catch an evanescent glimpse of my white hat left behind to mark the spot where the secret sharer of my cabin and of my thoughts, as though he were my second self, had lowered himself into the water to take his punishment: a free man, a proud swimmer striking out for a new destiny.' When he finished the story, he got up, said to the old man – who, like me, had listened impassively for more than two hours – that he would be back the next day. He bid me farewell with a nod of his head and left. I was at a loss. When the nurse came back, I asked her who my father's roommate was, and she said she had no idea, she was new on that wing. The night nurse could certainly tell me. That night, I found the head nurse on that floor. And she told me what she knew. My father was sharing his room with an eighty-year-old American, who had lived in Brazil for many years. 'He doesn't have anyone here, no relatives, no friends.' They were trying to find his son in the United States before he died. When his condition started to worsen, the old man had been sent from a nursing home to the hospital. He had cancer. His days were numbered. I asked who the young man was I'd seen that morning, if he was a relative. She said no, he was a care-taker, hired by the charitable institution that ran the old people's home where the man had previously lived, an institution founded by American missionaries. 'I think the guy has taken care of him for years,' the head nurse told me in the hall.

The next day, there he was, punctually, at ten. He opened the same book and this time started to read the preface of *Lord Jim*: 'One sunny morning, in the commonplace surroundings of an Eastern roadstead, I saw his form pass by – appealing – significant – under a cloud – perfectly silent. Which is as it should be. It was for me, with all the sympathy of which I was capable, to seek fit words for his meaning. He was "one of us."' He spent two hours reading to the impassive old man. I couldn't tell if the man could understand him or not. As on the day before, at the end of a chapter, he got up, said goodbye to the old man, and left. I went after him. I asked him how much the old man understood of these morning reading sessions – I wanted to know how much my father could understand of what I said to him. 'I always read the same things. The stories he liked the best. It's the least I can do,' the man answered, and left.

My sister arrived at lunchtime, as she had the previous day. I went out to walk around, to clear my head. She told me that she had an appointment at five, so she needed to leave in the middle of the afternoon. When I got back, I was alone with my father and the old man. Suddenly, for the first time since we had got to the hospital, the elderly American seemed agitated. He said things in English that to me seemed random and haphazard. I called the nurse, who gave him an injection of morphine. He slept the whole night. In the morning, the young man returned at the usual time and started on the next chapter of *Lord Jim*. Unlike the other days, however, the old man eventually started to get excited and say incomprehensible things, forcing the young man to interrupt his reading and go over to the bed to calm him down. The American argued with him, wanting to get up. From the little I could understand, he said he was expecting a visit, a person who could be there any minute now, without warning, someone he had spent many years waiting for. He demanded to be allowed to go to the door. The young man tried to get him to lie back down. I asked him if he needed help. He asked me to get the nurse. She came and gave him another dose of morphine, and he quickly quietened down. I asked the guy what the old man wanted, but he didn't feel like chatting. He repeated what I had already understood: 'He always says the same thing. He's waiting for someone who could show up at any minute. I even start to believe it and find myself glancing over at the door, thinking someone's about to arrive, and I get so distracted I can't even read.'

I hadn't slept for two nights. So it took me a while to wake up on the third morning. It took me a while to realize that I wasn't just dreaming those words. When I opened my eyes, the old man was talking to himself. They had tied him down so he couldn't sit up or stand. My father was still motionless, with his searching, open eyes, as if terror was all he had left. He couldn't even end his own life. I placed my hand on his sweaty forehead. He looked at me with his horrified eyes, but since he hadn't had any other expression for the past few days I couldn't know whether it was real horror that he felt or if that was just the last contraction of his muscles before his face had lost its ability to move. I ran a hand through his wet hair and went over to the other bed. When I drew the curtains separating the two beds, the old man looked at me with his glassy eyes, wordlessly. I asked him if everything was ok. He kept looking at me in silence. I repeated it in English. I asked if he needed anything, if he wanted me to call the nurse. He didn't move, but he did manage to mumble another noise, as if he wanted to say that everything was all right, or at least that's what I understood, or wanted to understand, at the beginning: 'Well . . .' When I closed the curtain, though, I heard a name behind me. He was calling me by another name. I opened the curtains again and asked him once again if he needed anything. And he repeated the name. He was calling me 'Bill', or at least that is what I understood. He tried to reach his arm out to me. I took his hand. He grasped mine with his remaining strength and started speaking English, with great effort, but at the same time in the happy tone of voice of someone who unexpectedly encounters an old friend. 'Who would have thought? Bill Cohen! Finally! Man, you have no idea how long I've been waiting for you.' Suddenly, he started breathing in a strange way. I felt nervous about all this, which I didn't fully understand. I kept asking if he needed something, if he felt bad, if he wanted me to call the nurse, and he repeated: 'Bill Cohen! Bill Cohen! Who would have thought! It's been so long!', every time with a bit more gravel in his voice, a bit less comprehensibly, as if his voice was coming from his bowels, as if someone was talking for him. 'Bill Cohen! What a prank you pulled on me!' And he was panting harder and harder. 'I knew you weren't dead!' It was the last thing he managed to say before his eyes rolled back and he started to convulse. I ran out of the room to get the nurse. When we hurried back, he was no longer speaking, only breathing laboriously. The nurse asked me to help her. We untied him from the bed. He was breathing with his mouth wide open, with increasing difficulty and with an increasingly frightening noise. His eyes open. I had never seen a man die.

The body was taken away early in the morning. The young man must have been notified, because he didn't come at the usual time. The next day I had already forgotten what the old man said to me in his agony. It was the day of my departure. My life went on. My father died three months later. I spent three years abroad. I have now been back in São Paulo for nine years. But it was only eight months ago, when I read the anthropologist's article in the newspaper, and when I spoke out loud that name that I didn't know but which somehow seemed familiar to me: 'Buell Quain, Buell Quain,' that I suddenly remembered where I had heard it before, correcting the spelling in my head, and discovered whom the old American in the hospital had been talking about, whom it was he had been expecting for so long. The realization troubled me greatly. I had to speak to the anthropologist. As I was trying to track her down, I called my sister and then the doctor who had managed to admit my father and who was now the director of the hospital. I had to find someone from the charitable institution who had taken care of the old American during his sickness, I had to find out who he was. The doctor gave me the contact information for the director of the old people's home where the American had spent his last years. It was fifty kilometres outside São Paulo. It was a single-storey house, surrounded by an arched veranda. The floor was made of cement covered with a smooth red wax. Everything was very simple. A very thin, white, and tall lady met me outside the house. We had talked on the phone, though I hadn't given her much information about what I was looking for. I just said that I was a journalist and I needed to speak with her personally. Her name was Mavis Lowell. She was wearing a mustard-green dress and she led me to the office inside the house. She had a strong accent. There were about four or five elderly people on the porch and in the garden. Only one looked at me when we walked by, and even he didn't look very interested. For the others, it seemed that either I didn't exist or they themselves were no longer there. They were uprooted. I tried to imagine what their lives had been like, how they were when they were young, the women they loved, their first loves, which is what I always try to imagine, and how they ended up there. I tried to imagine where the people were who loved them and who either no longer loved them or were dead. I asked if they were all Americans. Mrs Lowell said that at the beginning, when the home was founded, they were, but that now there were only a few left. On a corner of the lawn, a girl was reading to an old man beneath a senna tree. Mrs Lowell noted my interest in her reading. 'They're young people, interested in literature. Beginner writers. They're volunteers. They help the old people and for them – I mean, for the young people – it's very good too. After all, old people are a source of history. Isn't that what brings you here?'

'Sort of,' I said, without knowing where to start, when we went into the house.

'But you're a journalist . . .'

I assented with a nod of my head. We went into the room. She directed me to a chair, took her place behind a wooden table, and finally asked me how she could help. I said that I was looking for information about an old man who had lived here and who had died eleven years ago. As soon as I said what had brought me there she changed her tone and stood up, dry. 'If I had known, I would have spared you the trip. You people in Brazil are very rude. People's lives need to be respected. These are private matters. It's their business, and it's up to them and their families if they want to discuss it in public. We don't have any money, but that is no reason for us to invade the privacy of our residents. We don't need to lower ourselves for media attention.' I tried to argue every which way, in vain. Mrs

Lowell was already waiting for me with her hand on the doorknob of the open door. I had barely arrived and was already being kicked out. She was offended and disappointed. That was when I understood that she might have thought I wanted to write something about the institution, since I had introduced myself over the phone as a journalist, as a way to get in to see her. They were broke, they needed donations. They had been forgotten. She must have thought that I could be a means of helping her, until I said what brought me there. She asked me if I needed someone to walk me to my car. I knew the way. I left, annoyed at my own lack of skill in bringing her around and convincing her to reveal what I was looking for. Everything I could have learned had dissolved in a couple of seconds. I walked back past the old man on the porch who had looked at me as I went in. He wasn't looking at me now. I walked to the car and was about to get in, having already opened the door, when, turning back to the lawn, I saw the girl who had been reading to the old man beneath the tree. It was like a vision. I shut the door and went over to her. She was reading a story by Machado de Assis, in Portuguese this time, to an old man in light-blue pyjamas, seated in a lounge chair with a quilt over his legs. When she noticed my presence, she stopped reading and looked up, as if to ask what I wanted. She didn't seem very pleasant. Her dark brown hair reached the middle of her back. I quickly said that I was looking for someone who could read in English to a handicapped neighbour. I said the neighbour was willing to pay, if required. She looked at me for a second and then answered that she would look into it and give me a call. I left my number. She didn't give me hers. Now everything depended on luck. I recovered a bit of hope when she called me the next day and said she would do it. We agreed to meet in my apartment. I preferred not to say anything over the phone, after what had happened with Mrs Lowell. Only when I opened the door did I notice how short she was. Her hair was in a plait. This time, I was determined not to lose my chance. I wasn't going to take any risks. I made everything up, saying that the neighbour was sleeping just then and that she would see him next week, when the reading sessions would begin, three times a week, as we eventually agreed (on the evening of the day before the first appointment, I would call and say the neighbour had died during the night). We agreed on a price. I told her that I would pay myself, out of sympathy for the old man, since it broke my heart to see the old foreigner abandoned in a strange land. I said I'd never got over the time I'd seen an old American die in my arms, in a hospital, next to my father. I outlined the story for her, without giving any details or revealing my true intentions. I said there was a guy who read to the old man every morning and that I had been really moved by the sight. Before I could even ask who he might have been, she murmured his name: 'It was Rodrigo. I took his place at the home. He's the one who told me about it. He was a teaching assistant on a course I did at the university.' I pretended not to understand, and she came out with the guy's full name, saying that he was now

a translator for a chemical company. I made a mental note
of the name and we went our separate ways.

I wouldn't have recognized him. He had changed a lot.
He didn't remember me either, though he had a vague
memory of the roommate who had arrived in the hospital
room three days before the old American's death, 'somebody with a brain disease', my father. I couldn't pick the
guy out from among the other patrons of the bar we had
agreed to meet in. The last eleven years had been unkind
to him. He was fatter and balder, and was grey at the
temples. But he couldn't have been more than thirty-five.
I told him on the phone that I would be wearing a red
shirt. That was enough for him, seeing me lost and hesi-
tant, to point me discreetly to a table at the back. I didn't
beat around the bush. I told him the whole story. I needed
to be able to trust someone and I needed him to trust me.
He was immediately interested when I told him about the
anthropologist's article, so much so that he immediately
told me everything he knew about the old American who
had died in the hospital bed next to my father's. He was
a photographer, his name was Andrew Parsons, and he had
come to Brazil, probably before the United States entered
the war, around 1940. He never returned home. On more
than one occasion the old man had shown him photographs, from the thirties and forties, of a beach near New
York and a tribe of Indians, probably in the interior of
Brazil. 'When I started to read to the old people at the
home, he was the one I felt most comfortable with. He
was tall and quiet, an imposing presence. He didn't have

anyone here or anywhere else. Only after his death did his son show up. An employee of his had dumped him at the home and took off, probably with whatever money he had left. They kept him there out of charity, since there wasn't anything else they could do with him. When he got sick, the missionaries managed to get him admitted to the hospital almost as a favour. Like the rest of them, he didn't speak much. I read and he listened. Right at the end, when he was in the hospital, he interrupted me and pointed at the door: "Is he here yet?" Delicately, knowing that there was no sense to answering, I asked: "Who?", even if only to keep him alive and interested, which was the entire reason I was there with him. It was really sad. And he, who never spoke or only did so with tremendous difficulty, gathered all his remaining strength and said with perfect diction: "I've been waiting for him for years. Go tell them that they can let him in as soon as he gets here." I didn't move, and he would say: "Go, go on. I don't want them to keep him waiting." After that he forgot what he had said, closed his eyes, and returned to his usual detachment, or resignation. Among his only possessions was a suitcase full of photographs. At the beginning, I had only heard about the suitcase, since the old man kept it a strict secret and only opened it when he felt like it, and never when anyone asked him to. Only after several months reading him the same stories, his favourite ones, "The Secret Sharer" and *Lord Jim*, by Joseph Conrad, or the passage on the colour white from *Moby-Dick*, did he finally ask me to help him take down the suitcase from on top of his wardrobe. I don't know how much that book and that digression on white contributed to his desire to see the photos. He didn't let me see them all (and there were a lot of them anyway). He made a selection, and only handed me a few. They were pictures of Indians.' I asked him of what tribe, but he didn't know. 'There were also pictures of a group of young people on a beach. The boys had pieces of cloth wrapped around their waists. At one point, when he was showing me those pictures, he mumbled something in English, like "the most beautiful kids in the world", but I might have misunderstood. They were in fact very attractive pictures. He showed me some portraits of a lady – it might have been his mother – and of a girl, whom I imagined to be his wife, though it might have been his daughter or even his mother, in her youth. They weren't conventional photos. They were the work of an artist. When, right at the beginning, I asked him if he was a photographer, he was offended that I even had to ask. He said they were very old pictures, of a world that no longer existed. Once, he sat staring at a picture of a young man. The young man was wearing a bathing suit and a backpack, his hair was wet and his eyes wide with shock. He stood in a doorway which framed a light background. It was the first time I saw him smile, while he held the picture and repeated: "Well, well, well." He gave me one of those pictures. It was of an infant in arms. I asked who it was, and he said that it was him.' The man interrupted his story and smiled at me, his eyes downcast, while he took another swallow of his beer. As far as Rodrigo

knew, the old photographer had left a son in the United
States, who only showed up after his father's death, to take
care of the legal formalities and gather his belongings,
which were no more than the suitcase of photographs and
papers. I asked him if he knew what kind of documents
the old man kept in the suitcase. It was a random question, but I needed to find out something. I was shooting
blind. Everything had been given to the son. I asked if he
had any idea where I could find him. And, to my surprise,
he said he probably still had the address at home, in an
old notebook, since a year after the photographer's death
he had to give the son the picture of the baby, since the
old man had given it to him when he was no longer all
there, saying it was of him, and Rodrigo had forgotten
it among the pages of a paperback copy of *Moby-Dick*,
where he used it as a bookmark. A year later, he happened
to open the book and see the picture, which he thought
might interest the son in New York. He got the address
from the missionaries in the home. He said he would call
me when he got home to give me the address. That was
all he knew.

With the information in hand, I wrote to the photographer's son, in New York, in an attempt to learn more about
the old man's relationship with Buell Quain, if there was
one. At no time did I lose sight of the possibility, however
small, that it was all a figment of my imagination. I might
have misheard him, since the months leading up to my
father's death were particularly tense, and my head was

not entirely clear. I waited for an answer in vain. In the
meantime, my research led me in other directions: I dug
through the archives of Heloísa Alberto Torres, I went to
Carolina, I visited the Krahô. When I returned from the
village and still had no answer, in September, I thought
that only Quain's family could give me the missing pieces.
All I needed was to know what might have been in the
possible eighth letter, besides those he sent to his father,
to a missionary, and to his brother-in-law before he died
(why wouldn't he have written to his sister? Or had he
written an eighth letter to his sister?), and to see if there
was any trace of the diary that his mother said he always
kept. The eighth letter and the diary would explain everything. If they still existed, both could only be with the
family. Besides the father and the mother, who were dead,
there were the older sister, Marion, the brother-in-law,
Charles, and their two children, whose names I didn't
know. If the sister and the brother-in-law were still alive,
which was improbable, they would be over ninety. And
their children, the 'girl' and the 'boy', would be seventy-
three and sixty-nine, respectively, to judge by what I had
seen in a letter from Quain's mother dated 1943. The 'girl',
if she had married, would no longer have her father's name,
which would greatly decrease my chances of finding her.
The nephew was the safest bet, or his children or grand-
children. I tried every which way to track them down. On
genealogical websites, on people-search pages on the
Internet. Finally, after so many frustrated attempts, I
resorted to the most antique method of all: sending letters

to every Kaiser in the phonebook, in Chicago, Seattle, and the state of Oregon, the three areas where, I gathered from Quain's mother's letters to Dona Heloísa, Marion Quain Kaiser and her family might have ended up. There was no longer a single Quain in North Dakota, in any of the lists I could find. I picked out a few Quains in Chicago, Seattle, and Oregon, just in case, and sent them the same letter. Before this archaic endeavour, however, I put in a desperate call to a friend in New York who put me in contact with a television producer renowned for digging up things nobody else could find. She had an exotic name. She was the daughter of South Asians who had emigrated to Canada. We exchanged a few emails and we had already more or less agreed on a price and how much time she would invest (she worked for a television network, so she would have to work for me in her spare time), when, before the astonished eyes of the entire planet, two passenger planes hit and destroyed the two towers of the World Trade Center. The newspapers said the world would never be the same. The fact is I never again managed to reach the television producer. There was nothing else I could do but rely on the letters. I wrote more than a hundred and fifty to all the Kaisers and Quains I found in the phone books of Chicago, the Portland area, and Seattle. By an unfortunate coincidence, these letters arrived just as the United States was panicking over anonymous letters containing anthrax, sent via the US Mail to media and political personalities, and even to average citizens.

I still tried to reach the producer one last time, in

vain. The last straw came when the network she worked for turned out to be the first major media company to get a contaminated letter. It was opened by a female producer whose identity was not revealed, and who was undergoing medical treatment. Of the more than one hundred and fifty letters I sent, I only got about twenty replies, all by email, some friendly, some less so, but all denying any connection to the Kaisers I was looking for. I don't know if any of the individuals who got my letters suspected an act of terrorism upon reading my exotic, unfamiliar name, and turned me in to the FBI. I don't know if any of them failed to read my letters for that reason. I don't know if any of them really were related to Quain and simply preferred to ignore me for reasons I don't exactly know but can guess – suspicious of my true motives, determined to preserve their family's privacy, or simply uninterested in something that had been over and done with for sixty-two years, and that a strange and dubious South American journalist was now trying to unearth. What I do know is that when the letters started arriving in the television newsrooms and congressional and governmental offices at the United States with poisonous bacteria, I could no longer count on the post, as I had hoped, to try to track down Quain's relatives elsewhere in the United States. My hands were tied. By an unhappy coincidence, terrorism for ever removed the possibility that I could speak to Americans I didn't know for reasons that would now sound to them even more suspicious and unlikely.

That was when the letters started coming back. Twenty-one slowly trickled in, returned to sender. The last arrived in an unusual way, after two months and the words 'mistakenly sent to Malaysia' stamped next to the addressee's name. They had even sliced off part of the bottom of the envelope with a hole-puncher, as if somewhere along the way somebody had decided to examine its contents. I confess that for a moment, looking perplexedly at the returned letter, paranoia got the better of me and I began to imagine that the uniform, circular cut at the bottom of the envelope had been made not to examine its contents but to introduce something. I ran off to wash my hands and blow my nose.

Everything led me back to the photographer's son. After receiving no answer to my letter, I had temporarily put him out of my mind. For a while, I rested most of my hopes on the clues the anthropologist had given me, which at first seemed more promising. Only later did I exhaust those means of finding what I needed – which was what I, supposing that it really existed, referred to as the eighth letter, the document that could lend some meaning to the whole story and to the suicide. I had already found loads of material, but it always led me in circles around Buell Quain. I couldn't manage to penetrate to the centre of his despair. So I decided to go back in search of the photographer's son, this time personally. I wrote him one more letter, asking if I could come to see him. This time, despite all the paranoia in the US, he answered. And he sounded very reasonable, though he didn't offer to see me. He said that all he knew was that his father had gone to Brazil without any explanation right before the United States entered the Second World War. He had never again been in contact with the family, who concluded that he had either gone crazy or deserted the army. The first he heard of his father was when he was dying and the missionaries at the old people's home wrote to him. They asked him to handle the bureaucratic and legal aspects. He had never heard of an ethnologist, he had no idea who Buell Quain might be, and so he couldn't help me in my research. He had no documents that might interest me. He had nothing else to say and asked me not to contact him again. At that point, after months of digging through the archives, poring through books, and reading the notes of people who no longer existed, I needed to see a face, even if only as an antidote to the endless, bottomless obsession that was keeping me from writing my so-called novel (the justification I had used whenever people asked), that was paralysing me, making me fear that the reality would be much more terrible and surprising than I could imagine and would only be revealed when it was already too late, when the research was done and the book was published. Because now I really was ready to write a work of fiction. That was all I had left, since nothing else had worked out. My greatest nightmare was that Quain's niece and nephew might pop up suddenly, and I would learn that they had been right in front of my face the whole time, ready to hand me the solution on a silver platter. The

real reason for his suicide would turn out to be something obvious, and it would reveal my whole book's ridicu-
lous artificiality. The only sign that the family themselves
didn't know the reason for his suicide was his sister's
letter to Ruth Benedict, a month later: 'The fact is that
none of us will probably ever know, which makes it all
the harder for us to move beyond it.' Even that was no
guarantee that she didn't have her own reasons for hiding
the truth, or that she hadn't discovered it later. I needed
a real face. I needed someone who had had some rela-
tion, however remote, with the characters in the story.
Even if that person didn't reveal anything I didn't already
know, he could anchor me, tear me out of that limbo,
snap me out of that languor, drag me out of that pit of
unfounded suspicions. Nothing proved that the old
photographer had any relationship to Buell Quain, or had
even met him, besides the fact that he spoke his name
before dying – if that is what he was really saying. He
might have just heard of Buell Quain and got interested
in the story, as I had, and gone to Brazil to investigate
it, the same reason why I was now going to the United
States. I took the plane to New York knowing one thing
for sure: if I didn't find out anything else, I could at least
start writing my novel. I thought the photographer's son
could finally release me from the morbid curiosity in
which I was trapped.

The fiction began the day I set foot in the United States.
The edition of the *New York Times* given out on the plane,

19 February 2002, announced the Pentagon's new strategy: to spread news – 'false if need be' – through the international media, to use all available means to 'influence foreign audiences'. I hadn't been to New York for ten months. The last time had been five months before September 11. I hadn't seen the city without the towers. I couldn't approach the photographer's son out of the blue. He had already made clear that he didn't want to see me. I couldn't ring him and say that I was in the city just to see him. I needed to catch him by surprise. I needed to be patient. And I was prepared to be. I was ready to stay as long as necessary. I was determined not to miss my chance. I just hadn't thought my chance would come so soon or that it would be so easy. I cooked up a thousand plans. First of all, I had to know what he looked like, and I had never seen him. I knew more or less how old he was, since he was born before the photographer left for Brazil, which meant he was at least sixty-three. On the first afternoon after I arrived in New York, I went to his building, which didn't have a doorman. I reconnoitred the neighbourhood, I walked down the street in disguise, and after long hesitation decided to ring the intercom to see if he was home. I thought I would ring and then not say anything, just to hear his voice. A man's voice answered, a voice that didn't sound especially old, so it could have been his or, perhaps, his son's, which is when I thought I would make up a story, anything, that I was delivering a package – whatever. I needed to see him, even if I had to go and hide behind a car and watch him when he came down. I would observe

him from the other side of the street. I couldn't miss my chance. I asked for Mr Schlomo Parsons. It was him. And before I could say anything else, he buzzed me through and told me to come up. I was stunned for a few seconds, holding the door open without understanding what was going on, unable to move ahead. Finally, I went into the building and got into the lift. My heart was in my throat. When I got to the seventh floor, I went to the halfway-opened door at the end of the hallway, where a light was on. He heard my steps and called out that I could come in. The apartment was packed with objects and books, rugs and furniture. Three tall windows faced the street and the trees of the park, diagonally across the street. A yellow Labrador came to greet me, wagging his tail. His owner shouted from the bedroom that he needed my help. It was a white room, with bare walls. In the middle was a large mattress covered with rumpled white sheets, which took up almost the entire space. The afternoon sun came in through the window. Scholmo Parsons was sitting on one of the corners of the mattress, bent over a box filled with brittle papers, which he was trying to close with adhesive tape. Without lifting his head or looking at me, he asked if I had brought a trolley. 'It's very heavy. You'll never get it down without a trolley,' he said, before asking me to help him tape it shut. 'Let me take care of it,' I said, taking the initiative. Only then did he look at me, in silence. And he got up. He was tall and thin, with dingy white hair, angular features and tanned skin, sunburned, though it was the middle of winter. Now the Labrador was sitting

next to me. I ran the tape around the box. I reinforced the
more fragile edges. 'You're not American, are you?' I turned
to look at him. He didn't have the photographer's light
watery eyes. I still hadn't decided on the best approach. I
could try to act aggressive, or pious, or, if I had been clever
enough to think of one, I could toss off the question with
a joke. The only thing I couldn't do was be honest. I
couldn't tell him who I was or where I was from. 'Where
are you from?' And then, before I had time to think, as if
someone had stepped up and spoken for me, I told him
the truth. He narrowed his eyes: 'Brazil?' I confirmed with
a nod, already regretting it. I thought I'd lost everything.
I kept taping up the box. After a few seconds of silence,
which to me seemed like minutes, he finally exclaimed:
'You've got to be kidding!' He was confounded. 'Brazil! That
country is stalking me.' I smiled, acting like I didn't understand. I asked him what he meant and if he had ever been
to Brazil. 'I have. Unfortunately,' he answered. On any
other occasion, I would have left off after a remark like
that, but now I knew I was on the right track. I asked if
he had gone to Brazil for business. He looked at me, wide-
eyed and sarcastic. 'Business? That's a good one!' Now I
was determined. Uninvited, I had finally managed to get
into the house of the man I had been pursuing for months,
and I had managed to speak to him on my first afternoon
in the city. He asked why I had moved to New York, and
while I invented a long answer, pausing to reinforce the
box, faking a professional aptitude I obviously lacked, I
noticed that he was lonely, and really was interested in

what I might come up with. It didn't matter what I said. I could say anything, and it could make sense or not, as long as I didn't tell the truth. The truth alone would ruin everything. In five minutes, he had already told me a lot about the things he had put in the box, bric-a-brac that had belonged to an old friend who had moved to Chicago. I gathered that they had lived together. I think he was testing me. Eventually, he gave me his hand, introduced himself (as if I didn't know), and asked me for my name. I made one up. Ever since I had written my first letter to the photographer's son, his name had been in my head. It didn't fit. It sounded wrong, if it's possible for a name to sound wrong. Schlomo is a typically Jewish name, and Parsons, as far as I knew, wasn't Jewish at all. He laughed and explained: 'Story of my life. My mother seems to have had a weakness for Jews. Anyway, I never knew her. She died a few months after I was born. I think her family was Jewish, Ukrainian immigrants. But I'm not sure about that either. I never knew them. I was raised by my paternal grandparents.' Slowly, the story was starting to come together. He said he was fifty-seven, but I knew that wasn't possible, since he had been born before the war: he must have been at least sixty-three. He was lying about his age. Looking at him, you couldn't tell. It was quite probable. He had a strong presence and a well-made face. He must have been a good-looking man. He spoke generally about the old people. He must have noted that I was uncomfortable, so he decided to provoke me. He said everything was relative. He said that he himself, when he left home aged seventeen, had gone to live with an older man, who must have been as old as I was now. He asked how old I was. He acted shocked. He said I looked much younger. The older man he had gone to live with when he was seventeen was much younger back then than I was now. Everything is relative. I finished sealing the box and he helped me take it to the door. Before I left, he offered me a cup of coffee. I followed him to the kitchen. While he was washing his hands at the sink, he closed his eyes for a second to protect them from the light that was entering through the windows. For the first time, seeing him with his eyes closed against the winter sunlight, I experienced a kind of hallucination. From a certain angle, he looked like Buell Quain in one of the photos his mother had sent to Dona Heloísa, the same portrait the ethnologist had given to Maria Júlia Pourchet with a dedication on the back. He shut the blinds and smiled at me. He asked me what the matter was, I looked like I'd seen a ghost. I didn't know what to do. I wanted to get out of there, but I couldn't leave without finishing what I had come to do. I needed to stay in that apartment as long as possible – an insufferable idea – even if staying there didn't make the least bit of sense.

When he saw my discomfort, as I was sitting at the kitchen table, he said he had something that might be of interest to me, since I was Brazilian. He went to the living room and came back with a briefcase, which he opened on the tabletop. There was a pile of photos of Brazil in the fifties and sixties: rafts on a river that might have been

the Tocantins; the Rio Carnival; the Iemanjá festival in
Salvador; the old houses of São Luís; a panorama of Rio
de Janeiro seen from Sugar Loaf, before part of the bay
had been filled in; the inevitable foundations of the Ministry
of Education and Health Building in downtown Rio; the
Edifício Itália and the Copan in São Paulo, etc. He showed
me some pictures of Indians. They looked like Krahô, but
they might have been from any other tribe. 'My father was
a photographer. He spent his life in Brazil. These are
Brazilian Indians. Don't you recognize them?' I didn't want
to get on his bad side, and I didn't know if he was being
ironic, but there certainly was a paternalistic tone in his
voice. I decided to ignore his provocations. I looked at the
pictures as I tried to rein in my curiosity. I couldn't betray
my interest too clearly. I felt that he needed to talk, and
I forced myself to listen.

'Your father lived in Brazil?' I asked, as I examined the
photos.

'It's a long story. I never knew him. He abandoned us
right after my mother died.'

'Abandoned *us*?'

'I was raised by my grandparents. His parents. They
didn't like my mother and so they didn't like me either. I
was imposed on them.'

'Why did your father go to Brazil?'

'Nobody ever knew for sure. My grandparents never
wanted to talk about it. He worked for a newspaper. He
might have gone on assignment. Since he disappeared
right before the war and never returned, people thought

he had deserted, that he had decided not to come back when the war broke out. My mother died less than a year after I was born. She had galloping leukaemia, a very rare disease. That's what they told me. I never knew her either. My father left right afterwards,' he said. At that point he went to the living room and came back with a picture. 'Look. Here she is. It's the only picture I have of her.' It was of a slim woman, with dark circles under her eyes, a thin face, heavily made up, with her hair pulled back. She wasn't especially pretty. The nose was pointed. She was cross-eyed and had an indefinably strange appearance. A sad expression. He went on: 'My father handed me over to his parents and vanished. I always hated my grand-parents. When I turned seventeen, my grandfather called me over and said that there were a few things I needed to know. My grandmother was very passive. She was always in his shadow, listening to what her husband said. My grandfather had a piece of paper in his hand. I never understood if they had waited until that day to reveal something they had always known or if they too had been taken by surprise, like I was. My grandfather called my mother a whore, said she had always been good for nothing, that I was not my father's son and so there was no reason for me to continue living with them. I was the son of the bitch. Nothing they could have done would have surprised me, but I never could have imagined anything like that. I didn't think they would kick me out of the house. He was very angry, shaking and upset. I was speechless. He handed me the paper. It was addressed to me, but they had opened it and read it. There was no envelope or date. I thought they could have forged the letter. I didn't know what my father's handwriting looked like. They wanted to get rid of me and knew how I would react. I left that house for ever. I never saw them again. In the letter, my father said he wasn't my father and asked me to forgive him. He thought that now that I was a man I needed to know the truth. He said that he hadn't abandoned me, that my real father had died in the middle of Brazil when he was trying to come back to see me. I never exactly understood what he meant by that. He spoke as if they were two different people. He spoke of himself as if he were somebody else.' The photographer's son told me this while he was making the coffee. I could no longer look at the pictures in my hands. I couldn't believe what I was hearing. The Indians aren't the only ones who tell you what you want to hear, trying to get on your good side, as if there were no reality. He went on: 'I think he went crazy when my mother died and left for Brazil. That was a way of telling me he couldn't see me again. When he said that my father had died, it was a desperate way of asking me to forget him, of trying to shake off his responsibility.'

No longer able to control myself, I let out a gasp: 'No.'

'What?' he turned toward me, holding the coffee pot.

'No, nothing,' I said, shifting my glassy eyes from that face in which for an instant I had managed to see the face of Buell Quain, but which now bore no resemblance to the ethnologist's. I pretended to be interested in the pictures of the Indians. He continued telling me the story of his life, but I no longer wanted to know that after he left home he had gone to live with an older man he had met at a beatnik poetry reading in a Village bar; I didn't want to know that he started following this poet around to meetings, exhibitions, and galleries, to every bar and every studio where artists gathered to read their poetry; I didn't want to know the name of the poet he called Frank; I didn't want to know anything about his life. He recited a poem – 'From this day forth I am going to walk on the sunny side . . . I am turning the corner . . .' – as he served me coffee.

'Do you think my story is sad?'

'No, it's not that,' I said, with the pictures in my hands.

'What do you think of the pictures?'

'What do you mean?'

He got annoyed: 'Are they good or not?'

'They're excellent. It's incredible . . .'

'Wait a second. If you don't like these, I've got some others that are more interesting. I'll be right back,' he said impatiently, leaving a plate of toast on the table. The Labrador, who was sitting at my feet, followed him. The photographer's son came back with another briefcase. 'Just look at these. They said he wasn't my father, but unfortunately for him genetics leaves no doubt.'

The briefcase was full of pictures of naked men, white and black, outside, on a beach, or in a studio. There were a few from Brazil, but most of them had been taken in the United States. Nowhere to be found among them were the two yellowing portraits of Buell Quain, full-faced and in profile, that I had seen in Heloísa Alberto Torres's archives. There was nothing that proved a connection between Quain and the photographer.

'Like father, like son,' he said, laughing. 'What he really liked to do was take pictures of naked men. In the letter he sent me when I was seventeen, he called Brazil a "wretched country". If it was so wretched, why did he end up there? Why did he stay? I never heard anything else about him. I didn't know how to find him. I didn't have an address. I couldn't ask my grandparents. I was a proud, rebellious young man. I preferred to forget about him. I only saw him when he was dead.'

I didn't say anything more. He sat down in front of me. He made childish noises as he drank his coffee. Instead of taking normal sips, he sucked the coffee out of the cup. He ate with his mouth open and talked with his mouth full. Every once in a while he gave the dog a piece of toast. 'And you? I've only talked about myself . . .'

'Me, nothing.'

To my good fortune, when I went down with the box, the man from the transport company was just arriving with the trolley to pick up the delivery. Before he could touch the intercom, I opened the door and gave him Mr Parsons's box.

I decided to move forward my return to the next day. I wanted to leave on the first plane. I had nothing else to do there. Reality only exists if someone else is there to experience it with you. Flights to Brazil usually depart at night. Mine was at ten in the evening. I got to the airport early and was one of the first passengers on the plane. Ten minutes before takeoff a young man, blond, tall, and thin, came crashing down the aisle, his backpack bumping into the backs of the seats, heading towards the back of the plane. He arranged his backpack in the overhead compartment above my head and asked if he could sit next to me, in the window seat. He had curly hair, a hooked nose, and looked friendly, though very ugly. The plane took off at ten on the dot. We flew more than six hours without speaking. I couldn't sleep. Neither could the guy next to me. He was reading a book. His was the only light in the cabin. Everyone else was asleep. I couldn't read anything. I turned on the video screen on the seat back in front of me. Coincidentally, we were flying over the region where Quain had killed himself. That was when the guy next to me, for the first time, paused and asked me if his light was bothering me. I said no, I could never sleep on planes. He smiled and said he couldn't either. He was too excited about his trip to sleep. It was his first time in South America. I asked if he was going on holiday. He smiled again and responded proudly and enthusiastically: 'I'm going to study the Brazilian Indians.' I couldn't manage another word. And faced with my silence and my befuddlement, he turned back to the book he had just closed and began reading again. I suddenly remembered learning, on one of those television shows about ancient civilizations, that the Nazca of the Peruvian desert cut out the tongues of the dead and tied them up in a bag so that they could never return to torment the living. I turned to the other side, fighting my own nature, and tried to sleep, even if only to quiet the dead.

Acknowledgements

This is a work of fiction, though it is based on facts, real experiences, and real people. It is a combination of memoir and imagination – like every novel, to a greater or lesser degree. During the research that preceded its writing, I relied on the assistance of several people, starting with Mariza Corrêa. Without her, I probably would have never known of the existence of Buell Quain, and this book would never have come to be. I am especially grateful for the priceless assistance of Maria Elisa Ladeira and Gilberto Azanha, from the Centro de Trabalho Indigenista, in São Paulo, who took me to the Krahô, as well as to the Krahô who hosted me. I was also lucky to have the contributions and support of Professor Luiz de Castro Faria; Professor Antonio Carlos de Souza Lima and Flávio Leal, of the Library of the National Museum, in Rio de Janeiro; the employees of the Casa de Cultura Heloísa Alberto Torres, in Itaboraí; Sally Cole, of Concordia University, in Montreal; James Davis, of the Archives of the State Historical Society of North Dakota; Professor Margarida Moura, of the University of São Paulo; Sally Kuisel, of the National Archives, in Washington; Ernest Emrich, of the Library of Congress, in Washington; Ronald Patkus, of the Archives of Vassar College, New York; Ricardo Arnt; and

Professor Julio Cezar Melatti. None of these people bear responsibility for the contents or the final outcome of this work.

Photo credits

page 26: Buell Quain, archive of the Casa de Cultura Heloísa Alberto Torres – IPHAN

page 32: Claude Lévi-Strauss and Heloísa Alberto Torres, among others, in the garden of the National Museum, Seção de Arquivos do Museu Nacional/UFRJ